THE
FORGOTTEN
CHAPLAIN

OTHER BOOKS BY ROBERT LIVINGSTON

THE SAILOR AND THE TEACHER

TRAVELS WITH ERNIE

LEAPING INTO THE SKY

BLUE JACKETS

FLEET

HARLEM ON THE WESTERN FRONT

W.T. STEAD AND THE C ONSPIRACY OF 1910

TO SAVE THE WORLD

THE FORGOTTEN CHAPLAIN

ROBERT LIVINGSTON

THE FORGOTTEN CHAPLAIN

iUniverse books may be ordered through booksellers or by contacting:

iUniverse
1663 Liberty Drive
Bloomington, IN 47403
www.iuniverse.com
844-349-9409

ISBN: 978-1-6632-1637-3 (sc)
ISBN: 978-1-6632-1638-0 (e)

Print information available on the last page.

iUniverse rev. date: 01/19/2021

*Lt. George Fox – Lt. Clark Polling– Lt. Father John
Washington, and Lt. Alexander Goode*

http://www.kofc.org/en/columbia/detail/the-four-immortal-chaplains.html

*This story is dedicated to all chaplains who brought faith and courage
to the men and women in our armed forces during wartime.*

CONTENTS

INTRODUCTION

Happy Birthday, Kieran... If my math is correct, today is February 14, 2021 and you are sixteen. Wow! The years have really flown by.

My present to you is story I started writing way back in 2012. The story is called *Forgotten Chaplain*. What makes the story special is that (a) you are in it, and (b) it is about four brave men, who are known to history as the Four Immortal Chaplains. More about them in a moment...

In this story you are fourteen and staying with your Uncle Bob (that's me) and Auntie Lynn. We have two children in high school, Rachel (a senior) and Matthew (a sophomore). Why are you living with your youthful cousins? Your mother's fictional job requires her to be in Europe for six months. Don't ask me what's she's doing. I have no idea. It's just an author's ploy to explain your stay with the extended family.

Uncle Bob (again, that's me) is a reporter for the *San Francisco Chronicle* and is investigating what happened to the *USAT Dorchester* (United States Army Transport) on February 3, 1943 during World War II in the North Atlantic within a 100-miles of Greenland. The ship, he knows, was torpedoed and sunk by the *U-223*, a German submarine. He is aware of what the four chaplains did --- a Catholic priest, a Jewish rabbi, and two Protestant ministers. They gave away their life jackets and thick gloves to save the lives of American soldiers. He knows the four chaplains went down with the ship, sacrificing their lives to help others. What he doesn't know is this: was there a fifth chaplain who also sacrificed his life, but has been lost to history? Circumstantial evidence suggests such an unknown chaplain existed.

As I do my research the family gets involved. Your cousins decide to help their father. You join in with a little assistance from Auntie Lynn. Together you solve the mystery.

Kieran, I have always been fascinated by the "what if's" of history. If John Wilkes Booth's gun had misfired and President Lincoln had lived, how might American history have been different? If Albert Einstein had not written his famous letter to President Roosevelt warning of a potential German atomic bomb, how might the history of World War II been changed? If John Connolly, the Governor of Texas, had been killed and not President Kennedy on that terrible day in Dallas, how might American history been altered?

Of course, these what if's" questions cannot be fully answered. But they do tempt and provoke, and engender heated discussion and debate, especially if we are disheartened by the way things turned out. Nevertheless, it is fun to joist with history. We do so even though the actual events will have the last word.

Naturally, I hope you will enjoy the story as well as learn some history. Feel free to share your thoughts with others, especially your mother. She, I know, loves history.

Grandpa, 2020

CHAPTER 1

DAYBREAK

JANUARY 1943 – 5:00 A.M. – THE EAST COAST

The rain, which had fallen for hours from the darkened sky in torrents, was finally abating, becoming a clammy, dispiriting drizzle that soaked everything in the port like a wet blanket. The chunky, dark clouds, still ominous and threatening, continued to float above the frantic efforts of men and machines below as if some-how moored by an invisible anchor. A bone chilling wind whipped through the early morning, wrapping itself around the worn civilian and military workers and the long line of weary soldiers. The long night was almost over.

Giant shipboard cranes lifted large wooden crates from the ever-swaying pier, depositing their precious cargo of engineering equipment, construction materials, and food into the ship's bay. Aboard the ship, fatigued sailors jostled with the bulky boxes, steering them gingerly into the yawning hole, while below deck other tired sailors pushed and shoved the crates into their predetermined locations. Around the ship equally exhausted stevedores manhandled other crates marked *US Army*, even as they attached heavy chains and ropes around them before landlocked cranes hoisted the containers into the ever-lightening sky. The harsh grunting of the heavily dressed dockhands was accompanied by an occasional cursing of the Gods, in tandem with the squawking and squealing of chains and pulleys bearing the full weight of the indispensable cargo. Nothing, it seemed, was going quietly into the night as 1,000 tons of necessary supplies were loaded into the baleful blackness of the ship's hole.

A long row of drenched and disheartened soldiers bearing duffle bags and weapons moved slowly and quietly along the pier toward the ship. The men, fresh from boot camp and the most basic military training, had come from Camp Miles Standish in nearby New Jersey. They traveled in sealed railroad cars to this point of disembarking. Due to wartime secrecy and the ever-possible threat of German spies, the smoke belching train's windows had been covered, secured against peering eyes, and the men had not been told their immediate destination. Had they been told, without question disbelief would have ruled. *Staten Island, are you kidding me?*

The lead soldiers stopped at the gangplank where two officers dressed in black, slick raincoats, reigned. Each officer had a clipboard, which he sought to keep shielded from the lightening, but still incessant raindrops. He checked every soldier against his clipped manifest. Names were called quietly without expression, or any sign of recognition, just names and numbers stated flatly against the cold.

> *Ben Epstein – E 860-818-34*
> *Grady Clark – C717-439-03*
> *Vincent Fruselli – F 395-988-80*

Each soldier acknowledge his name and dog tag number with a quiet nod of his head, trying desperately to calm himself, to present to the officers at least outward confidence, to push back the nervousness and fear tucked away deep within his mind. The tightness of his mouth and the bleak, faraway look in his eyes gave him away, of course. He was embarking on a voyage to some already fixed rendezvous with an enemy of his country. He was, however, not going alone. The possibility of death, a tight knot in his stomach, was his constant companion as he eyed the shifting gangplank crunching against the pier, moved by the slapping of gentle waves and an insistent sea. Once aboard the ship, he knew, his destiny was locked into some yet unknown fate.

Aboard the ship and watching the scene below were two men cloaked in heavy sweaters and ponderous jackets, and tight woven woolen caps to ward off the chilling wind. Both men were Negroes. They watched in silence against the background of noise and controlled chaos as the loading of the ship proceeded. No words were spoken.

None was needed.

They had seen this spectacle before, indeed too many times. They knew what was in store for the men and ship. Another run across the barren, watery wastes of the freezing North Atlantic loomed. Another "cat and mouse " game with the damned U-boats lurking in the depths. Another throwing of the dice against the law of averages in still one more effort to beat the odds. All this they knew and acknowledged to themselves in unstated mournful sadness. Again, they would sail into the darkness besieged by German U-boats and only God to navigate them safely through troubled waters.

One was tall and heavyset, and not even his arctic garb could hide the presence of a strong physical body. His hands, wrapped in beaten leather gloves, were huge. They were the hands of a professional boxer who had fought endless rounds taking on all opponents. He had even slugged it out in an exhibition match with the great prizefighter, Joe Louis. Three exhausting rounds and then it was lights out and some decent prize money.

A woolen cap covered his head, which had once bobbed and weaved too often in the confines of the ring. A battered nose and a rock-hard jaw highlighted a kindly face, one almost spiritual in nature, which, a person could conclude, was totally out of character given his previous vocation. Had we been able to peer beneath his cap, puffed ears would have attested to too many jabbing punches received, if not telling left hooks and right crosses smacking against his face.

As a fighter he had gone under the name of "Big Hit Jones," a heavyweight fighter from a small rural hamlet in Mississippi. Now the Navy referred to him as merely Morris Jones, chief cook in the galley. But, to his friends he would always be "Big Hit," the man with the explosive right punch and excellent culinary skills.

A bulge in the big man's jacket suggested a weapon perhaps, and in truth it was sort of one, which he carried with him at all times, a copy of the *Holy Bible*, a gift from his mother the day he left home to find his way in the world. What had she said? "Always turn to the good book. Always." Over the years he had. It was well read and, beyond question, well worn. It served him often in the violent world of boxing and later as he learned out to be a cook, and in recent years aboard a lonely ship in hostile waters. He was not above asking for divine assistance, either in the 7th-round or when 1,000 meals needed to be served. "Lord, let me endure," was his mantra.

Turning to his buddy, who was standing with him on the promenade deck, he said, "Cookie, just look at them. Christ, they're so young."

Nodding, Cookie turned ever so slightly, and said with regret in his voice, "They're always too young."

"Yeah."

Cookie was an experienced member of the "galley slaves," the Negroes mainly, who cooked and fed the ship's crew and passengers. He looked nothing like his oldest friend. Slim and trim best described his pencil-like body, which not even a lot of heavy weather clothing could obscure. His real name was Abraham Freeman. He was from Knoxville, Tennessee. His mother adored the "Great Emancipator," and honored him by naming her first born after the slain president. In the segregated high school he attended, he had been a sprinter on the track team, an outstanding runner and hurdler, a "flash on the track," as he was described in the school's yearbook. A life in the kitchen of a cruise ship had produced a great baker, thus the appellation, "Cookie."

"How many times have we made this run?" Cookie asked as he unconsciously gripped ever more tightly the ship's railing.

"Eight times."

"How many lives does a cat have?"

"Nine."

Cookie shrugged and looked again at the long tine of soaked, bone-cold soldiers before saying, "Poor bastards. They looked scared to death under those metal pots."

"They have no idea how scared they're going to be."

"Yeah," he said with a great sigh. "Yeah."

Talk gave way to silence. Each man, lost in his own thoughts, held vice-like the hard, cold railing, which offered safety from the wintery waters welling up against the ship. The railing was immune to the fears and hopes of the men working and boarding, and offered no interest in the loading of the ship. It simply existed, neither compassionate or angry. It was devoid of passion. It was untroubled by emotion and sentimentality.

As always, numbers began to run through Big Hit's mind. He thought; so many men, so many days at sea, and so many meals to prepare before reaching Greenland. And then the questions: was there enough meat? Eggs? Milk? Flour? Vegetables? The list was endless. And predictably, the answers were always the same. So many stomachs equaled "X" amount of provisions for the seven-day run to Leif Erickson's adopted homeland. The refrigeration units were filled to capacity. Foodstuffs bulged in boxes and ship drawers. No matter what, stomachs would be full. The bounty of wartime America had provided.

"Figuring the numbers again? Cookie remarked.

"Got it down to the last can of beans."

"You always do. How many this time?"

"Over 900."

"Over?"

"902," Big Hit added flatly. "Exactly 902."

"More than last time"

"More construction workers this time, 171 civilians."

"For those bases they're building," Cookie muttered, at Bluie West One."

"Exactly 597 military personnel," Big Hit said. "To protect what's being built at that so-called secret base."

With that, they both suppressed with great effort a deep-throated laugh. They were content with smiles acknowledging some truth known to them.

"Damn," Cookie whispered, "what a hell of a place to fight the war. Christ, every German spy in Newfoundland knows what's going on? The Krauts aren't stupid."

"Knowing about it is one thing. Doing something about it is another."

"As you say, Bit Hit."

Having settled that issue, Big Hit completed his mathematical cadence. "And last of all, 134 crew members in good standing."

"When they're not drunk in some port."

"There's that," Big Hit, volunteered.

The two men were quiet for a time as they watched the last of the newly minted soldiers board.

"Wonder what they think of the ship?" Cookie shared with Big Hit.

"What would you think? Big Hit asked. "Just look at this old tub."

"Old tub indeed," Cookie snarled back at him in mock anger. We are standing on a graceful cruise ship, I'll let you know."

Big Hit turned away from his view of the pier. He admired the ship's super-structure. He tugged off his cap and squeezed out the rainwater before covering up his head and two oversized ears. The then gazed at the old girl, trying mightily to stretch his vision over the 357 feet of the ship, and to somehow take in the almost 6,000 tons of metal and wood.

"Remember Cookie, when we first saw her? What was it? 1936, I think," about a decade after she was launched."

"That was the year. In Boston, wasn't it? We were two black guys looking for a job."

"And we got one."

"Kitchen helpers, Big Hit."

"Cooks in time."

"It was the best job a Negro could get," Cookie sadly stated. "We cleaned the toilets. We cleaned the rooms. We cleaned the casino. We cleaned up everyone's mess. But in the end, they threw us into the kitchen, and we did learn how to cook for all those white folks taking a coastal steamer along the east coast."

"Boston, Charleston, and New Work," Big Hit added.

"Carried 325 passengers in fine style," Cookie reminded him. Even made the run to Bermuda a couple of times. Now that shore leave was good living. Sunny skies, cold drinks, and lovely ladies."

"She was a fine ship. She was so damn nice to look at, a luxury liner with graceful curves and sparking white paint shimmering in the morning sun. Now look at her."

"She was once the "finest hotel" at sea," Big Hit reminded Cookie. "There was once laughter, and music, and dancing into the wee hours."

"And the casino, where gambling and booze mixed with beautiful women, and very rich patrons."

"We had some good years," Big Hit stated with a little remorse. "It would be nice to have those years again."

The two men paused to gaze at the object of their affection. The white paint had given way to a wartime, drab grey color compliments of the War Department. The old ship was looking just that, very old and dilapidated, something for the junk dealer's scrap iron farm. Where card tables and slot machines had once jostled each other for space, now soldiers slept. Where once deck games had been played, now guns stood to fight off the enemy hiding beneath the waves or behind cotton-like clouds in the sky.

The old ship was no longer a sleek liner cruising the ports-of-call. Now she was a troop carrier ferrying men to far off bases, and registered to the Navy as the USAT --- United States Army Transport. She might be weather-stained and slow going, but she was their home, their lady of the sea.

As if awakening from a deep sleep, Bit Hit snapped, "We're US Navy now, God help us, and we've got meals to prepare, Cookie. Let's get at it."

"In a moment."

"What's on your mind, Cookie?"

"Did you notice those guys on the deck greeting each Army guy?'

"Yeah. What about them?"

"Who are they?"

"Officers. Chaplains, I think. We're carrying four of them."

"Chaplains, you say, Big Hit. That's good. A word from God can't hurt where this old ship is going."

"Amen to that, brother."

The two men drifted away from the promenade deck railing and disappeared into a stairwell leading to the ship's kitchen. As they did, they passed a lifeboat secured to the deck, which brought a fearful thought to mind. Throughout the loading of the ship, many of the stevedores had remarked about the slowness of the ship, her paltry few knots compared to an attack submarine cruising on the surface. They had heard the comment, "suicide ship." They took that crude prophecy into the kitchen with them.

It was time to prepare the morning meal.

At that very moment the first rays of a morning sun broke through the menacing black clouds and the slight drizzle finally abated. Daybreak. The sun's morning light found the ship's hull near the anchor hole to reveal one word, *Dorchester.*

https://uboat.net/allies/merchants/ship/2616.html

CHAPTER 2

THE VISITOR

JANUARY 1962 – SAN FRANCISCO

"Robert, I think he's here. A very large, official looking black Lincoln just parked in front of the house. Half the Congress could be sitting in the backseat. Are you listening?"

Standing in the master bathroom, Robert Samuels didn't respond immediately to his wife's inquiry. He was gazing intently into the mirror, which gazed back at him with a questioning look. He fussed a moment more with his hair, brushing hard-to-control waves into some sort of obedience. He checked his face, checking for puffs of shaving cream, which had avoided the warm towel he used after shaving. He checked for nicks. It would be unfashionable to meet his visitor with blood streaming down his cheekbones. After all, it wasn't even an election year.

"Robert, did you hear me? Dark suited FBI-types are getting out of the car. They seem to be checking out our house and the neighborhood. Please tell me you haven't been writing unpleasant things about the White House."

If nothing else, his wife, Lynn, was insistent. Samuels knew she would keep after him until he answered. Still, he needed another moment to check himself out. After all, it wasn't everyday a government personage from Washington visited an average citizen for Sunday breakfast. Quickly, he checked his starched light blue

9

shirt and pleated dark blue pants, compliments of the Market Street Emporium. No tie today. Sunday was for an open collar. Next his eyes roamed to his shoes, dark black and highly polished. Finally, he checked out his specialty looks beginning with the generous smile, then the severe questioning persona, and finally, the "I got it face." Everything was in order, he hoped, for his surprise guest.

He looked, he thought, like a successful, high-powered news reporter, which, of course, he was, enjoying his Sunday with time off from the daily beat. It didn't hurt to indulge in a fantasy, he commented to himself with a half-smile.

"Half the federal bureaucracy is headed our way. I'm sending the kids up if you don't answer."

Samuels knew his wife would sic the kids on him. All three of them, Rachel, age 17 and Matthew, two years younger, and their cousin, Kieran, age 14, would hunt him down and, given their youthful energy, tug him downstairs against all resistance. It was time to respond. The Canadian Mounties had nothing on these heartless creatures when they were on the prowl.

"No need. I'm coming."

As Samuels entered the kitchen, the doorbell rang and three unchecked, zealously, youthful spirits bolted for the front door. He stood back and watched the kids blast past him in a mad dash to see who could get there first As he waited, he realized that his wife, Lynn, his post-war bride of almost 20-years, was standing next to him.

"Any thoughts, dear?" she asked with just the hint of a smile.

"Not one."

"We paid our income taxes?"

"Yes."

"You haven't given state secretes to the Soviets?"

"Not a chance."

"Well then…"

The door to their home, located in the middle class Richmond neighborhood of the city, opened to reveal a tall, imposing man in his mid sixties dressed to kill in a dark black Brooks Brothers suit, a black tie torturing his neck, and highly polished black, wing-tipped shoes. He was the very model of a government official, or possibly a funeral director. Samuels couldn't decide which would be better. He assumed an answer would shortly be forthcoming.

The imposing unknown visitor stood in the doorway while his stoic, unsmiling aides stayed outside, vigilant in the early morning mist. The visitors smiled. In one held a lovely spring bouquet of colorful flowers, and in the other a dark brown leather briefcase, which was well worn. News reporters have an eye for details. With a slight bow he handed the flowers to Rachel, saying, "For your mother." And with that he passed over Samuels' threshold, glanced at everyone and announced, "I'm Dan Kurtz. You must be the redoubtable Robert Samuels. And, of course, you're Mrs. Samuels. And I take it these are your children, Rachel and Matthew. And you are?"

"Our relative, Kieran," Rachel blurted out, pushing her shy cousin forward to shake hands. Kurtz smiled and said, "A pleasure, I'm sure."

It was obvious to Samuels that Kurtz had done his homework. Probably a dossier on the family, complete with photos. Not even a used car salesman was as glib and prepared as this guy. He was too prepared. The hairs on the back of Samuels' neck began to strut and a little voice bellowed, "Watch out."

Kurtz next shook Samuels' hands vigorously and then turned to the teens in one fluid movement, and with a smooth voice said, "Hi guys. Perhaps you would like this." Deftly Kurtz removed from his now open briefcase three obviously first edition classic comic books enclosed in a clear plastic covers: *Terry and the Pirates, Archie and His Friends, and The Phantom*. This was an immediate hit with the kids who took to their gifts like a polar bear to ice.

This guy was better than good, Samuels thought to himself. His strutting hairs were now marching in cadence with the little voice, which was on full alert, blaring out a repetitive warning, "Something is up." Interrupted by husband, Lynn announced to one and all, "Breakfast."

As to the meal, it was great. Lynn really poured it on. Waffles made with a special recipe handed down from her mother and sausages, honey-soaked, along with scrambled eggs. Real butter graced the table and real Vermont maple syrup, not the fake stuff. Hot chocolate and fresh brewed Colombian coffee topped things off. All this was devoured to small talk, Kurtz's flight from Washington D.C., the local weather, how the Giants were doing, how the kids were doing in school, and a few questions about investigative reporting. Innocent talk but certainly not the reason for Kurtz's presence. Samuels had the feeling that these were just the preliminaries to something more substantial.

After helping to clean up after breakfast, the kids departed with their reading materials, leaving the "old folks" alone with three refilled coffee cups.

"Great kids, "Kurtz volunteered. "They are so full of energy and excitement, if I do say so. I guess they are like a reporter, energized and excited as doors to the past are opened unearthing mysteries hidden by time. What do you think, Mr. Samuels?"

What did I think? Something is in the wind, I thought. I'm being said up. Not quite the pig on the spit, but close.

"At times, yes."

Talk about being noncommittal.

"Great," Kurtz replied. "I hoped that was your view. I guess you're wondering why I'm here."

What an understatement! His question, however, brought us back to the business at hand.

"The thought has crossed our minds," Lynn said in a half humorous manner. We don't often get such calls from the White House, especially from the Chief of the President's Staff."

That was Samuels' Lynn. Get to the heart of the matter. Besides her good looks and sharp intelligence, and certainly her cooking, there was still another reason why Samuels loved her. She was a no nonsense type of person with great legs. Tough to beat that combination, he reminded himself. How could he not fall for her?

"Yes, I'm sure it did," the visitor said. "Well, let's get down to it."

Let's," Samuels said in agreement.

Kurtz opened his brief case and pulled out a large file marked *"Security File #1"* in *large bold black print*. We were impressed; it was much better than being *Security File #123.*

"Mr. Samuels, you are the author of *Miracle at RP 10*, are you not? And, if my memory is correct, a second book entitled *Miracle at Pusan.*"

"I pleaded guilty. *Miracle at RP10* was about a destroyer, the *USS Aaron War*d, that survived kamikaze hits off Okinawa in '45."

"An excellent book. I read it, as did the President. He loved the stuff about the anchor and chain, how the father of one dead sailor bought the anchor and chain after the war."

"He placed it in front of the VFW Building in Elgin, Illinois to remember his son."

"Who wasn't even eighteen, right?"

"Yes."

Beyond the sadness of the past, Samuels was really impressed, as only an author can be. President Kennedy had read his book. Wow. This was turning out to be a great Sunday. He looked over at Lynn with a big, dumb smile, which she returned to with a "Don't let your ego get out of joint, mister," look. She was right, of course, but the President had read his book.

"The President, I might add, has also skimmed through your latest effort about the heroic stand of our forces in Korea in 1950 to protect the Pusan Peninsula, to end the North Korean advance. 'Damn good book' was his comment."

"Not many people realize how desperate the situation was in the first months of the war. The North Koreans came close to pushing us into the Sea of Japan. It was a close call."

"Which the President believes you recalled with historical accuracy and a penchant for details."

Lynn's look notwithstanding, my ego was bursting. JFK had checked out my newest book. Again, wow. That's cool. The little voice and strutting hairs seemed to be standing down. Samuels was feeling pretty good about things. And fair was fair. Samuels had read the President's book, *Profiles in Courage* years ago. He had particularly enjoyed Kennedy's chapter on the Edmund G. Ross, an all-but-forgotten Senator from Kansas, who saved President Andrew Johnson was being impeached in the aftermath of the Civil War. Folks in Kansas at the time weren't happy about that vote. They almost drove the Ross family from the Jayhawk state. Many years later Kansas honored Ross for his political courage.

Though Samuels never admitted it, Kennedy's book had touched a sensitive cord. He was always drawn to people who exhibited ethical courage in the face of overwhelming odds, when they had done what was right regardless of the personal consequences. Samuels always wondered if he would display the same courage if the opportunity arose.

Reality came home when Lynn asked, "We're happy the President has good taste in what he reads, but why are you here, Mr. Kurtz?"

Kurtz sipped his coffee, carefully replaced the cup, adjusted his tie, and leaned toward us with large imploring eyes.

"The President, Mr. Samuels, needs another *miracle* from you."

CHAPTER 3

HILL AND BRADY

DECEMBER – 1961 – KNOXVILLE, TENNESSEE

Approximately a month before Robert Samuels received his visitor from Washington, two older men in their early 50's sat down for lunch on Oak Street in a rib joint claiming the "best BBQ in the South, " or at least the Volunteer State. The boast was audacious, very much like the owner, a charming former quarterback for the University of Tennessee football team, who passed his way to glory including a visit to the Sugar Bowl on New Years Day. After going pro, he carved out a career in the restaurant business with an emphasis on honey-covered ribs cooked in buttery fat. As to whether his ribs were the best, well that was a matter of taste, if not region. The folks in Memphis competed for the title, as did the good people of Chattanooga.

"What are you going to have? Mr. Hill, " a waiter familiar with the two men, asked as if he didn't know.

"The usual, Pete."

"And you, Mr. Brady?"

"The same."

"Drinks?"

"Two gin and tonics," Brady answered. "And very light on the tonic."

The waiter left in a whirl with their order. To other patrons, the two men appeared comfortable in their setting, probably successful lawyers, or bankers given the conservative, well-fitting blue suits they wore, which were offset by thin ties escaping down their necks against stark white shirts. Appearances, though, could be very misleading.

"Christ, Hoover must really be pissed at us this time," Brady, the taller of the two, snapped.

"Being farmed out isn't bad," his companion responded, "especially for old guys like us sneaking up on retirement."

"You like Knoxville?"

"Lets say, I don't dislike it," Hill said. "Hell, it could have been worse. The Director could have shifted our butts to Anchorage."

"Well at least they have good ribs in Knoxville."

At that moment, their waiter arrived, announcing his presence with a flourish of well-practiced words. "Your drinks, gentlemen. Light on the tonic, ribs coming."

Again the waiter hastened off leaving the two men to consider their fate.

"Do you think it was our criticism of *COINTELPRO*, which led to our transfer from San Francisco?" Brady asked.

"You know damn well it was," Hill said, but the criticism was deserved. What a name for a domestic surveillance unit to spy on civil rights group, including the Southern Conference of Christian Leadership and King himself. Insane."

"COunter INTELligence PROgram… What a name! What a stupid program," Brady offered. "Spying on dissidents, college kids. Hell, investigating ministers."

"Spoken with the passion of a good Catholic with whom I'm in total agreement. Unfortunately, our master didn't agree with us."

"J. Edgar Hoover!"

"Never state the obvious."

"Not the first time we've been in the soup," Brady added.

"But it's good chicken noodle soup, as my Jewish mother would say. And Kosher, too, if prepared just right."

"Almost as good as my mother's Irish stew or corn beef."

The two men exchanged knowing grins. They loved talking about food and their checkered professional resumes.

Their careers in the Bureau had been punctuated with less than stellar moments, when, perhaps a little too often they had been too outspoken voicing dissenting views. In the FBI bureaucracy questionable behavior was not a good way to be promoted. Certainly this was true when the Director had denounced Dr. Tim Howard, a surgeon in Mississippi, who dared to criticize the FBI for failing to solve the murders of George W. Lee and Emmett Till, two civil rights activists. Where others had followed the "party line," Hill and Brady had been less than enthusiastic. While not a career ender, their behavior marked them as less than fully supportive of policy. For this reason, they were ostracized to Knoxville.

"Knoxville is better than Siberia," Brady stated matter-of-factly.

"Better food here, too. Reindeer steaks don't do anything for me."

Their waiter arrived with fanfare, announcing for all to hear, "Your lunches, combination ribs and salad, and a smattering of baked beans, and a side of garlic bread. Enjoy."

"I'd yell at the guy," Brady said, "but he's the owner's brother-in-law."

"How'd you know that?"

"I'm a FBI agent."

"Aren't we all," Hill replied.

The two men dug into their meals. Beans and salad lent themselves to the etiquette of knives and forks, but ribs were best grabbed, two-handed, and devoured in a manner appropriate to the carnivore nature of these federal agents.

"Great food," Hill said.

The two men had shared many meals together, beginning in 1937, when, as raw recruits, they first joined the Bureau. They had met in Quantico, Virginia, following the war and college. They bonded immediately. The tall, freckled face Irishman with the hearty laugh enjoyed the dry humor of his lean, olive skinned buddy. Brady had attended Notre Dame, a school befitting his ancestry. Hill graduated from UCLA, a good school for a Jewish kid. Both were political science majors. At Quantico, they took a 21-week course of study to become agents. They passed with superior marks. When World War II broke out, Brady was assigned to Army Intelligence, Hill to the Navy's version. Their war records were excellent. Brady was part of the team, code named *Operation Paper Clip*, which brought German rocket scientists to America. Hill participated in gathering intelligence for Project Olympia, the planned invasion of Japan in early 1946. Two atomic bombs erased the need for that attack. After the war, they returned to the Bureau.

"Outstanding," Brady announced as he finished off the last rib. "The beans were really tasty."

"Not bad for Siberia," Hill said with a smile.

The waiter arrived with coffee, Tennessee Brew #1, made from a choice Bolivian bean, or so he said. No cream. No sugar. These customers took their coffee undiluted and steaming hot even in the hottest weather. No dessert competed with the bean.

"Let's get down to it," Hill said.

"Right."

"You know what the Director said.

"I was with you when we visited his office," Hill replied.

"Well?"

A week ago, they had flown to Washington. In the hallowed halls of the FBI Building, Hoover had instructed them in his office.

"It's bull shit, but the Kennedys want it done," Hoover hissed. Bobby going to send Kurtz, his Jew friend, to San Francisco to see this guy, a reporter for that liberal rag, the *Chronicle*."

As always, Hill flinched inwardly when the Director spoke this way of Jews. It was no secret Hoover was uncomfortable with minorities. The few Negroes, Jews, and Hispanics in the Bureau were a testament to his need for an essentially white only, Protestant and Catholic law enforcement agency. It was more than reluctance on Hoover's part. It was ill-disguised resistance.

"That Attorney-General wants us to keep tabs on this reporter, if he accepts an assignment from Kurtz. He wants us to protect this reporter's backside. I'm assigning you two to this case. You're out of purgatory. Wherever, this guy, Samuels, goes, you follow. I want daily reports. Got it?"

Hill and Brady got it.

"What's so important about this guy?" Hill asked.

"He's nothing. But he'll be researching something. That's what's important."

"What?" Brady questioned.

"No concern of yours now. Maybe later. Just keep me informed."

"Will be in the dark," Brady explained.

"You'll live. And one more thing, don't screw this up. You're too close to a well-earned pension," Hoover remarked sarcastically.

The agents got the message.

"I repeat, what are we going to do?" Brady asked.

"We're going play it close to the vest. See what happens. Figure out what's going on," Hill grumbled.

"Our usual "M.O."

Hill shrugged.

"Time to go," Brady said.

"Too bad, another coffee would be nice."

The two men paused in their conversation and then, without warning, Hill asked, "Did you know that Knoxville was the underwear capital of the United States until a few years ago?"

"Really?"

"Indeed. Twenty textile mills were once the city's largest employer."

"And you know this, how?" Brady asked.

"I'm a trained agent."

"Well, Mr. Agent," Brady said, "let me ask you this. What has Knoxville got to do with the National Gallery of Art in Washington D.C.?"

Shrugging his shoulders, Hill said, "I haven't the faintest."

"This town used to be called the "Marble City." There were

quarries all around the area producing pink marble, and that material was used in constructing the National Gallery."

"And how do you know all this?" Hill asked.

"Army intelligence."

"Ah."

The two men got up, dropped a few bills and loose change on the table and prepared to leave. As they did, the waiter appeared. "I trust everything met with your approval."

"Beats reindeer," Hill said.

CHAPTER 4

A MORAL ISSUE

JANUARY – 1962 – SAN FRANCISCO

Robert Samuels wasn't sure he had heard Kurtz correctly. He gazed at him with a "what in the world are you talking about?" look. "Another miracle?" Samuels asked. "Perhaps you'd like to elucidate." It was his habit to use big words when he was nervous. And he was very nervous.

"Of course," Kurtz replied." That's why the young Kennedy sent me here.

"Robert Kennedy?" Lynn gasped. "The President's brother?"

"None other," Kurtz confirmed quietly.

"The cute one," Lynn divulged and the tough one in the Justice Department," she added in a more serious tone. "The 'hatchet man' for the President."

"Perhaps we could leave it at this; he gets things done for his brother."

"Like taking on the mob and Castro," Lynn said matter-of-factly.

"Like that."

Samuels was at a loss. He wasn't paying attention to Kurtz or his wife. Other things were on his mind. Why would the government's number one law enforcement official send Kurtz to see a reporter?

"What do you want, Mr. Kurtz?" Samuels asked, perhaps a bit too sharply. "In newsroom parlance, what's the scoop?"

"You are being offered an opportunity to serve your country, Mr. Samuels."

"Go on," Lynn nudged. "How is my husband going to serve his country? Not in uniform, I trust."

"Of course not. He's already done his fair share. Simply put, the Kennedys want you to write a book."

"Write a book," Samuels repeated incredulously.

"Exactly. You do write books, don't you?"

"I think we've established that, so what's up?"

"You must research a subject, a historical topic, if you will, and complete the project by the 1ˢᵗ of January, 1963, about one year from now."

Write a book! What was this all about? Samuels thought. True, I've written a couple of books for military buffs, but at heart, I'm just a newspaper hack pounding out the hash of daily life in the city, and occasionally, if the editor was generous, a more serious investigative report.

"What subject? Why the deadline?" he asked none too politely. "Anyway, I can't do it. "I already have a job. Whatever you want must be rather important. But get someone else. How can I take off work for a whole year?"

"You can because you're the 'chosen one,' as far as the both Kennedy's are concerned."

"But…"

"There are no problems. The folks at the *Chronicle* have agreed to give you a paid leave for exclusive rights to the story, which you will submit to your editor as the narrative develops. And once the book is written the *Chronicle* at syndicating the story in so far as it wishes. In fact, they look forward to publishing the book, perhaps even backing a Hollywood film. Does that alleviate your concerns?"

"They really agreed to all that?" Samuels asked with amazement. "Damn."

"Really," Lynn mused. "There must have been a lot of arm twisting."

"It's amazing what a call from the Oval Office can do," Kurtz said with a knowing, pleasant smile.

"But paid leave," Lynn spat out a bit sharply. "What does Robert have to do, kill someone?"

"No, nothing like that. But he will have to travel a great deal, to Germany and possibly Newfoundland, and Greenland, plus a few Southern states and ..."

"Jesus," Samuels gasped. "Sorry about the interruption, but that's a hell of a lot travel."

"The government will, of course, provide the necessary passports, and cover all transportation and accommodation costs, and all expenses related to your research. You will find your budget very generous."

"How nice," Lynn said cautiously. "And all of this is legal?" she questioned in her most charming voice.

Kurtz looked at her with disbelief. "Naturally. And secretive, I must emphasize. Only a select few will know about the assignment. You will, of course, be able to submit stories to your editor that touch on your research but you cannot divulge the purpose of it."

"And as to the purpose, the justification behind all of this, I assumed we shall soon learn?"

Disregarding her husband's question, her patience having finally ran out, Lynn asked, "Not even our kids?"

"Just point out that Dad is simply doing research for the White House. You can keep them informed, but as to the purpose, it's better to avoid sharing."

"You do want him to kill someone," Lynn spat out.

"No, I want him and you to watch a short film."

Without missing a breath, Kurtz got up and walked to the front door leaving us wondering where all of this was going. "Just one moment" he announced without any fanfare before opening the front door. He waved to his car. A few minutes later, two tall, very muscular secret service-types entered the house. One carried a box by its strong, black plastic handle. A dark blue suit cloaked him and a tight crew cut sat atop a face, which gave nothing away. The second man, who was dressed and groomed in a similar fashion, followed. He was carrying a movie screen. They were as stoic as ever.

"With your permission, Mrs. Samuels..." Kurtz remarked

pleasantly, "Joe and Bill will set up a projector and screen in your living room."

"Of course. Make yourself at home."

Joe. Bill. What names! They were almost as good as Smith or Mr. White. You might as well call them Mr. X or Mr. Blank. And whom was Kurtz kidding? Permission to show a film; what a line Samuels thought. Who's going to tell an envoy of the government and his two, very large bodyguards, "No, you don't have permission." Anyway, Samuels wanted to see the film. His curiosity had been aroused. His reporter's instinct him was beginning to itch.

Joe and Bill set things up expertly. They closed the drapes and dimmed the lights. They did all this in complete silence. Kurtz ushered Samuels and his wife into their living room, where they sat down at his urging. He remained standing.

"A few weeks ago, the President was on national television appealing to the public for support of his proposed civil rights legislation. You probably saw him."

"We did," Lynn said quickly.

"And?"

"We were impressed. Even the kids were moved by it," she added.

"We had quite a family conversation as I recall," Samuels pointed out.

"Did you know that the President received the final draft of the speech only minutes before airtime? Ted Sorensen was making changes right up to the red light."

Really? Samuels marveled. "That close."

"The President was prepared to speak extemporaneously, and did so a couple of times."

Samuels was immensely impressed. Few politicians ever diverted from a carefully prepared script. It took "political guts" to stray from the teleprompter.

"You've got our attention. What now?" Samuels asked. As if one cue, the projector whirled into motion and the film started. The President of the United States was addressing the Samuels household and millions of others.

We are confronted primarily with a moral issue (today). It is as old as the scriptures and is as clear as the American Constitution. The heart of the question is whether all Americans are to be afforded equal rights and equal opportunities. One hundred years of delay have passed since President Lincoln freed the slaves, yet their heirs, their grandsons, are not fully free. They are not yet freed from the pains of injustice. They are not yet freed from social and economic oppression.

Samuels had heard the President speak again, and, as before, he considered the speech one of the best Kennedy had ever given. And he agree with the young president. Jim Crow laws and segregation throughout the South had to be ended. Under Abraham Lincoln the nation couldn't remain half-slave, half-free. "Old Abe" understood that. Under President John F. Kennedy, the nation couldn't remain Jim Crow in the South and more liberal in the North. Something had to give. America needed to avoid some form of South African apartheid taking root throughout the country, locking the society into a system of segregation and discrimination on the basis of race. Kennedy had accepted this challenge.

And this Nation, for all its hopes and all its boasts, will not be fully free until all of its citizens are free. Now the time has come for this Nation to fulfill its promise. The fires of frustration and discord are burning in every city, North and South, where legal remedies are not at hand.

The President was so right, Samuels thought. Our cities were social tinderboxes ready to explode in a violent urban storm. Something had to be done, and quickly. Racial injustice was devouring our national mythology that a good education, fairness, and hard work were an open road for all our citizens regardless of ethnic or religious background.

A great change is at hand, and our task, our obligation, is to make that revolution, that change, peaceful and constructive for all. Next week I shall ask the Congress of the United States to act, to make a commitment it has not fully made in this century to the proposition that race has no place in American life or law."

That was it, Samuels knew. The President was proposing a new civil rights bill, which, if enacted such legislation would begin the process of dismantling discrimination, whether sponsored and supported by southern statehouses, or permitted through de facto traditions in the North. In all its forms, discrimination, prejudice, and bigotry ran contrary to Thomas Jefferson's credo that "all men are created equal."

The lights came on as the project blinked out. The drapes were opened and Joe and Bill quickly repacked and left the house. They were efficiency in action. Only then did he see the kids, Matthew, Rachel, and Kieran.

"I like the President," Rachel said with youthful honesty. "He's cool."

"Me, too" Matthew added. "He's a good guy."

"I'd vote for them," Kieran said with enthusiasm.

It seemed that the President already had three supporters.

"You saw the whole film," Lynn declared. "I thought you were upstairs."

The kids shrugged. "We were, mother, until the lights went out." Rachel responded calmly. "We were curious."

"What's a moral issue?" Matthew asked. "Kieran asked me."

"Good question," Samuels replied, "one we're about to get answered, right, Mr. Kurtz?"

"Indeed, but your daughter has asked a telling question, don't you think?"

Samuels was caught up in a familiar family dilemma; that is, what was the thin line separating "adult talk" from a more open family discussion. Perhaps too quickly, he resolved it expeditiously, but not necessarily appropriately.

"Scram you three, go to the movies or something. My treat. Enjoy yourselves. We'll talk later."

"Dad," Rachel said in a way only teenagers can, half sarcastically, half imploringly, half critically, and half beseeching, "Is discrimination a moral issue, which must be fought?"

To everyone's surprise, Kurtz answered Rachel and in the process took Samuels off the proverbial hook. "A moral issue challenges our basics beliefs, young lady. It forces us to consider what is good, what is evil, and what our stance will be. It forces us to decide what we will champion. Isn't that right, Mr. Samuels?"

The kids were staring at Samuels. Lynn was looking at her husband. Kurtz was gazing at the reporter. Outside, Joe and Bill were probably listening on a "bug" they left in the house. Sunday morning had brought Samuels a lot of attention.

"Yes, we must champion what is right. We must follow our conscience."

"Always?" asked Rachel?

"As much as possible. Consistency is important. And difficult..."

"Is that like a 'moral compass,' Kieran asked?"

"Where did you pick that up?"

"From you, Sir, as far as I can remember.

Silence prevailed for a moment. Though he was a bit flushed, Samuels took advantage of it. "Kids, off to the Coronet. There's a new Robin Hood movie playing. Here's a ten spot. Enjoy the cokes, popcorn, and Milk Duds. Take the old Ford."

"Dad," Rachel pleaded.

"We'll talk later when I know more about Mr. Kurtz's visit."

"Promise?"

"Go."

And they did.

Kurtz said, "You're lucky. Those are really special children."

"We know," acknowledged Lynn.

"But they were getting to you, Mr. Samuels."

"They were asking tough questions, Mr. Kurtz."

In this lull, Samuels tried to take stock of things. The film ignited any number of questions about Kurtz's visit, but strangely, the most immediate one dealt with Samuels himself.

"Why me? There are lots of good writers around?"

"Four reasons. First, you seem generally sympathetic toward the President Kennedy's policies. We've reviewed your articles in the *Chronicle*. Very fair minded, even when you disagreed with the Administration. Second, You're a good reporter. You dig for the facts. You work hard to find the truth. You don't seem to have an axe to grind beyond getting at the truth."

"That's you, Robert," Lynn chimed, "to the last letter."

The "truth shall set you free." The thought passed through Samuels' mind, paused and moved on. How often had he heard that phrase in his college journalism classes? How difficult he had found applying this dictum in his work. The truth was elusive. It was not always convenient. And it could unleash a storm of anger, not just approval. Truth had an ugly side. To deal with truth you needed sharp elbows.

"Third, how should I say this? You care about your country. Perhaps more strongly, you love this land. You are guilty of sentimentality. To use an old-fashioned word, you are a patriot, my friend."

"And you know this how? Samuels retorted.

"Your "miracle books" give you away. You admired service and sacrifice by the citizen soldier and his counterpart in the Navy. You stressed the virtues of duty, honor, and country."

Samuels was listening, but his eyes had fastened on a framed photograph on the fireplace mantle. It showed the *USS Aaron Ward*, trim and deadly, its flags unfurled, and its banners blowing in the wind as it cut through the sea. Samuels knew that the photograph bore Admiral "Bull" Halsey's signature for a job well done. Next to the photograph was an American flag, rolled up and contained in a triangular shaped wooden frame. The flag had been a present from the V.F.W. to thank him for his first book, *Miracle at RP 10*. Samuels' eyes rested on it for a moment before moving on to a framed letter from General Matthew Ridgeway, commander of UN forces in Korea, who congratulated him for his second book, *Miracle at Pusan*.

"Okay, I'm a patriot," Samuels snorted. "So what?"

Kurtz didn't respond to Samuels' question. Rather, he finished his list. "Fourth, and possibly the most important reason, you tell a good story. You make contact with people. They like to read what you write."

"He does that," Lynn confirmed. Now what is it you want him to do?" she asked again, this time with no hidden impatience.

Kurtz went to his briefcase and withdrew an envelope with the words, "For Robert Samuels" written on it. A signature was below the words, John F. Kennedy.

"This is for you," Kurtz said. The President wants you to tell the American people a story about something, which happened almost twenty years ago on February 3, 1943 at precisely 12:55 a.m. off the coast of Greenland."

Samuels held the envelope in his hands. It was so light. It was if he was holding air. He noticed that they were quivering a bit. Intuitively, he knew that the envelope, once opened, would shape his life in the coming months. Lynn moved closer to him, saying, "Open it, Robert." And he did, so very carefully, very slowly and peered inside. An absolute look of wonder embraced his face. "What on earth?"

He removed the contents, a single United States postal stamp.

CHAPTER 5

THE COURTHOUSE GANG

A few miles south of Nashville is a small town, which prides itself on southern hospitality and big-city amenities, Franklin, Tennessee. Set against a landscape of rolling green hills and meandering rivers, and shady areas of new growth trees, the town named after Benjamin Franklin is a lovely family-oriented place to live. Founded October 26, 1799, Franklin was once the center of the plantation economy in the state before the Civil War, and for this, it paid a heavy price on November 30, 1864. On that day, which many call the bloodiest 5-hours of the war, over 8,000 casualties gave testament to the severe fighting. The city was almost destroyed. Today that battle and the town's past is celebrated and remembered in local museums, Civil War sites, a walking tour past Victorian homes and the largest privately owned Confederate cemetery in the country.

In the center of Franklin is a stately old courthouse dating back to the 1850's. Built of brick and wood in three sections, each with a triangular roof, the building is the center of the town's political and commercial life. The middle section has a large bell tower rising from it. The glistening white paint stands in contrast to the heavy red bricks, which seem to glow a fiery red in the afternoon sun.

Patriotic red, white, and blue bunting hung from second and third story banisters on most days in mute acceptance of the "lost cause."

Deep inside the courthouse in what is called the basement area, there are many rooms, now mainly used to house legal records and commercial documents relevant to the town's history. One room, number 1861, however, has a different purpose. Town lore suggests that more than one murder was committed in this room in addition to political deals cut late at night. Many believe that election results were "altered" here over the years due to recounts. Stories abound of politicians and their mistresses meeting in the seclusion of 1861 to discuss matters of the heart. That long-winded poker games fed by an always full bar took place here was an accepted fact of life in Franklin.

Entry into Room 1861 in more modern times was limited to "loyalists," defined simply as men belonging to the Democratic Party, who believed in the segregation of the races in order to maintain "white rule." The status quo reigned in this room.

On this particular day, late in the afternoon, three men were in the room. They were enjoying Old Crow straight bourbon while speaking in conspiratorial voices and smoking large burley cigars from Cuba, which had found their way past the silly sanctions placed on imports from Castro's island. The three men were religious, god-fearing souls who belonged to the local Baptist Church. They were patriotic men, each of whom had volunteered for service rather than being drafted into World War II. They were family men, who loved their wives and spoiled their children. They took their marriage vows serious. They were also segregationists and honorable members of the local branch of the KKK.

The fellow with the big belly and hairless dome was known as Baldy for obvious reasons. In high school, he had been a tough offensive lineman who plowed ahead, determined to reach the end zone. He owned the local Ace Hardware Store, the Remington Gun Shop, and the NAPA auto supply store. It was his view that "Baldy can fix it or shoot it."

The guy with the long legs was Stretch, all 6 foot 6 of him. a former basket-ball player for the University of Georgia, who won all-conference acclaim. He was the President of the First Franklin Bank and Franklin Investments. He was the savvy man with money in town. He liked to say, "I'll help you save it, buy it, or speculate with it."

The third man was known as Nails. He didn't look like a construction man. No bulging muscles. No tobacco spit clinging to his lips. No metal helmet on his head. With his horn-rimmed glasses, he looked more like an engineer, which was indeed his professional calling. His game was golf. He owned the Top Dollar Construction Company, which always seemed to have the lowest bid when contracts for public works were awarded. His company was big in school construction and road maintenance. He was fond of his company and enjoyed saying, "I can dig it, build it, or blow it up."

The three men had other things in common. All were born in Franklin in 1923. All came from the town's best and most affluent families. All had great grandparents who had fought in the Civil War and not too far from the city of Franklin itself, Vicksburg and Chickamauga. All had relatives who had suffered indignities during the period of "reconstruction" imposed upon them by the federal government, when good people felt the sting of Northern occupational soldiers, and black politicians in the state house. And all had family members who joined the first KKK movement in the late 1870's to end the Negro franchise and to reassert white authority in society.

The fathers of the three men had answered President Wilson's call to arms during the Great War in 1917-1818. As doughboys, they fought in France against the Hun. Upon returning home, they went to school or joined in the family businesses. They also joined the second wave of KKK activity during the 1920's, which now was violently anti-Jew, Catholic, and segregationist. They claimed, however, never to have participated in lynching's, only other less drastic extra-legal activities. They raised their boys to be good citizens and to accept the notion of racial superiority.

As for the three men in question, they eventually took over the family businesses after World War II, even as they joined the third wave of KKK activity in the 1950's, which had contempt for the "Earl Warren Court's decision to end "separate but equal" school facilities. This new wave of Southern anger pounced on atheists, homosexuals, and intellectuals. It attacked the civil rights movement and its non-violent, leader, Martin Luther King. It took no delight in the Catholic Kennedy brothers in the White House. Its heroes were "Bull Connor" and George Wallace.

Their political battle cry was simple. "Leave us alone. If you want to live next to Negroes, do it. But don't force us."

Now they were meeting in Room 1861 to discuss a problem.

"What did your Washington source say?" Baldy asked Stretch.

"Something happening."

"What?" Nails asked.

"Kurtz is visiting a writer, a newspaper guy in San Francisco."

"Who's Kurtz?" Nails asked sharply.

"A special envoy of the Kennedys."

"Jews and Catholics … Crap. What we have to put up with," Nails grumbled. "What a world."

"Big deal," Baldy responded.

"He's being given an assignment."

"To do what?" Nails asked.

"To research the "fifth man theory.""

The three men were aware of the idea of a "fifth man," who died with the Four Chaplains on the *Dorchester*. They also understood the implications, if indeed a particular fifth man existed and if he was black. In their KKK branch, they had been assigned the task of hindering any effort to validate that theory.

"What happens now, Stretch?" Baldy asked.

"We observe."

"And?" Nails asked.

"We do our assignment."

"Starting?" Baldy questioned.

"Now."

Baldy and Nails knew something was in the wind. Stretch hadn't told them everything. But he would.

"We're going to California."

"California," Baldy gasped.

"Northern California to be more exact," Stretch reminded them. "Some place called Weaverville. It's in Northern California."

"Why?" asked Nails

"Because that's where the Source believes Kurtz is going to send the reporter," Stretch said.

"Why, Baldy asked?"

"To see some photographer."

"We know this because?"

"Inside information. Very inside."

CHAPTER 6

THE FIFTH MAN

JANUARY 1962 – SAN FRANCISCO - NOON

Robert Samuels felt awkward, even a little silly. In his hands he held the thin, very small stamp by its edges. No note accompanied it to explain its importance, possibly its purpose. Without doubt, the stamp conveyed some meaning, but what? That was the question.

"A postage stamp," Lynn said. "A three-cent unused stamp. See, Robert, no cancellation marks."

"You're right," Samuels said agreeably.

"Maybe the government thinks we're so poor we can't even afford a stamp," she quipped.

"I don't think that's the case. Look at it more carefully."

Focusing more intently, Lynn saw what Robert was talking about. The stamp, colored in dark grey and black, showed four faces above a ship, which was obviously sinking into an angry sea. Edged into the stamp were the words, *"Interfaith in Action."*

"How could this stamp," she wondered aloud, "have anything to do with the President's sense of urgency concerning his civil rights legislation?"

They both turned to Kurtz. "Time to fess up," they said in unison. "No more games."

"You're right, of course. It is time. Please sit down and give me a few minutes more of your time. In a moment you'll understand everything."

"The clock is running," Samuels said under his breath and none too warmly."

Kurtz reached into his briefcase, his bag of tricks bag and brought took out a thick folder and a large brown envelope, magazine size, which was marked Robert Samuels in heavy, bold print.

"Do you know what the stamp portrays?" Kurtz asked.

"I've heard the story of the four ministers who went down with their ship after it was torpedoed," Samuels said curtly. Who hasn't? They were known as the *Immortal Chaplains.*"

"A small somewhat technical correction, if I may. One was a Catholic priest, another was a Rabbi, and two were ministers, Dutch Reform and Methodist, I believe. And yes, the stamp, as it is shown, indicates they were immortalized as chaplains."

"I stand corrected," Samuels responded. "But a German U-boat did sink them. I'm sure of that."

"Right. The *U-233* to be exact did the dastardly deed about 150 miles from Greenland and safety. Over 700 men died as the troop ship sank. The *Dorchester's* fate"...

"My God," Lynn wailed. "So many lives."

"It was a troop ship, loaded to the gills, every space crammed with young soldiers, Kurtz reminded them. "Only about 200 survivors."

He paused to let the deadly math sink in on Samuels and his wife before going on.

"Back to the stamp, what else do you see?"

"Three words," Lynn barked out --- *"Interfaith in Action."*

"Precisely. Four men of differing theologies acting together in faith for a noble cause."

Samuels suddenly remembered. "The four chaplains gave their lifejackets to others. They stayed aboard the ship and were last seen praying as the ship slipped beneath the waves."

"An heroic act of self-sacrifice, was it not?" Kurtz asked.

Samuels and Lynn could only nod in agreement.

"The ship was the *USAT Dorchester*, a United States Army Transport, and it was torpedoed on February 3, 1943 after midnight at exactly 12:55 a.m. as I mentioned earlier."

"Almost 20 years ago," Samuels volunteered."

"Yes."

"The anniversary will be next year."

"Quite right."

"You want me to write a book coinciding with the sinking."

"To a degree, yes."

"Mr. Kurtz, you're hedging."

Kurtz paused. For the first time, Samuels saw that the man seemed emotionally exhausted, as if he was bearing some great weight still unshared with others. After a moment, he continued.

"The President hopes the book, your book, might encourage Americans to approach our racial problems with greater compassion for all men, and on an ethical basis in order to move past merely legalistic questions. He wants this story of self-sacrifice to move us beyond a segregated, discriminatory America. And he needs your help to do this. He needs this story to fend off the many critics and outright enemies of the proposed civil rights legislation."

"The pen is mightier than the sword," Lynn announced.

"In my case my old Underwood typewriter."

"Either way, Mr. Samuels, the President is betting on you to deliver. Point of fact, the President has even suggested a title: *Miracle at Sea*. Naturally, this is only a suggestion. You're the boss."

"Actually, my editor and the publisher are the real bosses here. Be that as it may, the title is catchy."

"You'll do it?"

"This is that important to the President?"

"Yes."

Samuels considered what had been said. In his own mind, there was no question he would help the President. But he did have a few questions.

"I assume a great deal has been written about the *Dorchester*. Why can't you use that material? Why a new book? What's te catch?"

"Information, there is, but not a story to stir people as the White House would like. Plus, we have some new information, which, hopefully, you will research."

"New information?"

"Yes. I mentioned the J.F.K.'s critics. He's got them coming out of his president ears, if I may say so. The Democratic Party is split on the Kennedy's proposals. The southern wing, extremely conservative, wants to maintain the status quo, a segregated society. Northern democrats are open to an incremental approach that doesn't destroy the party as in '48 when Senator Hubert Humphrey tried to have a civil rights plank. The Southerners walked out and ran their own candidate. The President needs a united party for what he wants to do."

"Of course, that makes perfect sense," Samuels replied. "He'll need every vote he can get."

"Absolutely. And do you know what he wants to do?"

"Civil rights?"

"In a general sense, yes. Specifically, he wants to use the equal protection clause of the Fourteenth Amendment to eliminate discrimination in all public areas or, if you will, public accommodations, including restaurants, amusement facilities, and retail stores. He wants to use the Fifteenth Amendment to protect the right to vote, regardless of race or color. Along with this, he wants to end discrimination in the work place. And finally, he wants to enforce the Supreme Court's decision in *Brown vs. the Topeka Board of Education.*"

"The Southerners will fight him every inch of the way," Samuels cautioned. Every damn inch."

"Not just the South. Republicans of every ilk are concerned about the over-expansion of the federal government, especially where education is involved. The cynics believe they don't want the black vote going to the Democrats. Others, even more cynical, believe the Republicans want Kennedy to succeed, thus giving the Grand Old Party an opportunity to inherit the white vote in the Solid South."

"Complicated," Lynn said.

"Very. And possibly dangerous."

"Why?" Lynn questioned. "What are you talking about?"

Samuels knew what Kurtz was getting at and, heart of heart he didn't want Lynn to find out. She might fear for his welfare if he took the assignment.

"Have you ever heard of 'Bombingham,' Mrs. Samuels?"

"No."

Reporters hear things. They see things. They connect dots. It's part of the job. Sometimes it's a heart-warming story that leaves you feeling good and hopeful about the future. And sometimes it's ugly, so sickening, and beyond human understanding unless savagery is somehow the new norm. All this passed through Samuels' mind after Kurtz's question to Lynn.

"A little exposition for Mrs. Samuels. Over 40 Negro homes and churches were bombed in Birmingham, Alabama during the 1950's. Physical violence was used to stop Negroes from exercising their constitutional rights to vote and to end discriminatory practices. People were intimidated, beaten, and assassinated with the not so subtle support of politicians and law enforcement. Did you ever hear of the 15-minute rule?"

"No," Lynn said, speaking in a tense tone.

When the Freedom Riders came to Birmingham, Bull Connor, the Police Chief, gave the 'red necks' fifteen minutes to beat up those college kids from the North. Then he had his police stop the battering. Guess who was carted off to jail for disturbing the peace? Not the bullies."

"Christ," Samuels cried out, "the white supremacists were encouraged to use violence. They knew no charges would be forthcoming. Nice system for bigots."

"Nice system for bigots," Kurtz said, anger coating his words. Behind almost all the agitation and violent resistance to social change and the advancement of Negroes was the KKK, the Ku Klux Klan, our fellow citizens. President Kennedy has to deal with those people, too."

Kurtz stopped talking. Samuels could see he was emotionally played out, totally drained.

"Would you like some water," Lynn asked. Coffee? Something stronger?"

"Some water, please."

Lynn moved quickly to the kitchen, turned the tap, and a moment later gave Kurtz a cool glass of water. He drank it slowly. As he did, Samuels said, "Excuse me for asking, but do you have personal interest in the *Dorchester* beyond speaking for the White House?"

"Your reporter's instincts?"

"A necessary curse."

"And a necessary virtue, I think."

"Your personal interest, Mr. Kurtz?"

"I'm from the South, Mr. Samuels, Knoxville, Tennessee to be precise, a great place to live. My family was in the furniture business. They raised me within the Jewish tradition and like many black people. I felt the pangs of bigotry more times than I like to remember. But unlike most Negroes, I could, if necessary, disappear into my 'whiteness' to escape from anti-Semitism and the charge of Christ-killer. Just change my name to throw off the haters. You know, let Kurtz becomes Kingman, and keep a low profile. When I wanted to, I could pass as a Christian with strangers, a well-educated WASP affiliated to conservative causes. I could emphasize my German heritage, not the Star of David. I honed these skills over time. Perhaps now you understand why I so strongly support the President. In short, I could pass as just one of the guys. Others couldn't."

"I feel there is something more, Mr. Kurtz."

"You are a bulldog, Mr. Samuels."

Kurtz sat for a moment, measuring it seemed, what he would say next, how much more he would share.

"A relative of mine was aboard the *Dorchester*. Army. He had trained at Camp Miles Standish and was headed for a secret base in Greenland. He wanted to fight the Nazis. Being Jewish made the war personal for him. He never made it. Drowned in the North Atlantic that terrible night years ago. Who knows, perhaps one of the Chaplains would have given him his lifejacket. Who knows? How ironic, yet appropriate that would be given what I'm up to these days."

"You said there was new information."

Kurtz reached I into his briefcase once more and brought out a typed sheet. He read directly from it.

"Seventeen affidavits were taken by the Army from survivors

after the *Dorchester* sank. Each statement was a first hand recollection of what took place in the final moments before the ship sank. Each one supported what the chaplains did after the ship was torpedoed."

Kurtz then proceeded to read.

> ***Henry H. Arnett*** *– "I knew the four chaplains and saw them give up their life belts and go down on the ship without them."*

> ***Thomas W. Myers, Jr.*** *–"I saw all four chaplains take off their life belts and give them to soldiers who had none … The last I saw of them they were still praying, talking, and preaching to the soldiers."*

> ***James A. Ward*** *– They were singing songs, hymns. I knew they couldn't get off. The next time I looked, it (the ship) was slipping away under water."*

"Those chaplains were special men," Lynn said, marveling at what she had heard.

"Extraordinary men," Samuels said, seconding his wife.

Kurtz handed the typed sheet to Samuels and the large folder, plus the brown envelope. He also gave him a white card.

"Read over the other statements. They provide a living testimony to the courage and conviction of the chaplains. As to the white card… You can reach me at the number on it, night or day. Use it, if necessary. Everything you need to get started with your research is in here."

"And the new information, which still remains elusive?"

"There is some evidence, much of it highly circumstantial, but all very intriguing that a fifth man was with the chaplains, and that he also gave up his life belt, and prayed with them, and died with God's name on his lips. If true, we will need to revise our history and print a new stamp.

"Mr. Kurtz, there must be more to this than a postage stamp."

"There is. If it could be proven, the President's plea for social change might have greater appeal to all fair-minded Americans in both the North and South. If it can be determined beyond a shadow of doubt in time for the 20th anniversary of the *Dorchester's* sinking, it might be just enough to enact a civil rights bill next year."

Samuels was perplexed. It didn't make sense. "How could," he asked Kurtz "one additional chaplain, or possibly a soldier or member of the ship's crew make such a difference?"

Smiling Kurtz said, "Suppose the fifth man was a Negro."

CHAPTER 7

THE FIRST STAMP

FEBRUARY 1962 – WEAVERVILLE, CALIFORNIA

Robert Samuels had been on the road for over five hours, driving first across the blood-red Golden Gate Bridge blazing in the early morning sunlight, then northward along Highway 101 through Marin County and past the turnoff to the wine-rich Napa Valley. He had stopped in the Clear Lake area for a hamburger and French fries, and a cool, thick strawberry milk shake before continuing toward Garberville, a small hamlet in the coastal Redwoods some two hundred miles from San Francisco. He still had another seventy miles to go before settling into his motel room in Eureka, the town, which described itself as the "Queen City of the Ultimate West."

As he drove, he reflected on his current state of affairs. Here he was motoring in a new 1962 Ford four door sedan, sparkling in its spanking blue paint job and US government plates. And it was an automatic. Just throw the gears into "D" and drive. No down shifting was necessary. No playing with the clutch. Just drive. And the Ford had air-conditioning, though such a luxury was of little use on "101" where fog and a Pacific breeze cooled off the road in addition to the shadows cast over cars and trucks by the giant redwoods. Talk about other amenities; the car had an AM-FM radio, which was great if you liked western cowboy music with a tinge of country thrown in once you neared Garberville.

Kurtz had kept his word. "The government will provide you with a vehicle and a gas card, and a voucher for your motel accommodations."

"A late model car?" Samuels' asked. "And an automatic?"

"You do drive a hard bargain."

"I can stay at the Hilton?" Samuels inquired, a teasing smile on his face.

"No. Something more modest, since the taxpayer is paying for all this."

"My food allowance?" Samuels once more questioned.

"A reasonable per diem, even for a reporter."

Kurtz had also given Samuels a point of departure, a place to begin his research. "In Weaverville, there's a photographer who can help you. I've contacted him and he's agreed to meet with you."

"Why?"

"Why what, Mr. Samuels?"

"Why do I need to meet with him?"

"You recall what was in the envelope?"

"Of course, one stamp."

"Precisely."

"You were persuasive, I assume in arranging this meeting?"

"Very much. And he was curious about your research. Just call him at this number."

"Okay, Kurtz. Only one more question; where's Weaverville?"

Kurtz took out a map and pointed. "Here," he said. And that's how Samuels found himself on Highway 101.

Two hours later Samuels pulled into the Redwood Inn, a mile south of Eureka. After signing in and unpacking, he attacked a large ham and sausage pizza at a local eating joint, finished off a tossed salad, smothered in mushrooms and diced olives. Two cups of black coffee settled in along with a large chunk of apple pie. Fully fed, he was ready to call home from his room. He was already missing his family.

He never saw the two men who followed him back to the Redwood Inn. He wasn't expected to.

"Hi honey. Guess who?"

"My intrepid reporter–husband?" Lynn asked.

"Right as usual."

"Well, tell me about your adventures today."

"Not much to tell after I picked up the classy redhead hitching a ride to Oregon."

"You didn't."

"Right. No nerve."

"My hero. Anything else to share?"

Samuels told Lynn about his drive, the redwoods, the towns he passed through, and the foods he ingested. She was very impressed by the coastal vistas and the great trees, but less so by his choice of food.

"How are the kids?" Samuels asked.

"Rachel is in love with a new student in her Algebra class."

"Again?"

"Again. Matt made the baseball team."

"Good. He can wait awhile for girls."

"Like his father?"

"I'll overlook that one. How's Kieran doing?"

"Adjusting to our home. Of course, he misses his mom, but he understands why her work takes her to Europe."

"Just one semester."

"True. Still, he had to move to San Francisco, and to a new school."

"He's a good kid."

"Right. And guess what?"

"What?"

"He's interested in being a reporter. He likes what you're doing."

"Really?"

"Truly."

"I need to raise his allowance."

"And the others, Robert. They're on salvation wages."

"That bad?"

"Worse. Now, as I asked earlier, anything else to share?"

"I miss you, Lynn."
"Already?"
"Yes."
"Good. I miss you, too. Stay safe, Robert. I love you."
"Ditto."

The next day Samuels began the 105 miles drive from Eureka to Weaverville along Highway 299, a twisting road that followed the Trinity River through steep V-shaped canyons. The Trinity was fed by melting mountain snow, which was abundant each year. His mind was now concentrating on meeting the unknown photographer, the first important step beyond his initial research.

For almost one month following his acceptance of Kurtz's offer, he had read everything available about the Four Immortal Chaplains: magazine stories and newspaper articles, the official Navy report on the sinking of the *Dorchester*, and all known accounts by survivors of that terrible night. He had carefully read the formal German reports of the sinking. The resources of the *Chronicle* had been used to unearth anything. It was fair to say he now had a working understanding of what happened on the *Dorchester.* He also had, as they say, a ton of unanswered questions. And most importantly, at no time had he come across anything clearly substantiating the presence of a "fifth man." Intriguing hints, yes. Actual proof, not yet.

Samuels entered Weaverville from the west and proceeded down Main Street before reaching Highway 3. Along the way he passed the Weaverville Drug Store, the oldest pharmacy in continuous operation in California. Stark brick buildings dating back the gold rush a century earlier dotted the town, which referred to itself as the "Mountain city in the Trinity Alps." He drove by the Joss House, the oldest Taoist temple in the state. Nearby he paused to look at the Temple of the Forest Beneath the Clouds, which was the oldest continuously used Chinese temple in California. Having read a little about the town, he understood now why James Hilton, author of

Lost Horizon, had been strongly inspired by Weaverville's mountain location to claim it as his mythical Shangri-La.

Samuels' research had also acquainted him with the story of "John-John," a Chinese laundryman who had become the laughing stock of a miner's camp back in the 1860's. Apparently John-John would do laundry for nothing and was seen by the miners as stupid, a person to be taken advantage of by smarter folk. But they didn't really know John-John, who would carefully wash loose gold dust out of the pants cuffs and shirttails of the miner's clothes. Over a few years, he accumulated sufficient "dust" to become a wealthy man. If there was a moral to the story, it was to be careful of perceptions. They can often be wrong.

As Samuels turned northward on Highway 3, he wondered if his quest for a possible "fifth man" was another John-John story. If so, however, perhaps there was gold dust yet to be mined in this story.

A little over two miles from Weaverville, Samuels turned off the road in front of a beautiful A-framed cabin completely surrounded by a lavish redwood deck. He could see that the cabin, which seemed mainly constructed of large glass window- panes. The cabin was built over a series of large granite boulders and faced the river to the west and the snow-packed Trinity Mountains. The view, Samuels imagined, was fantastic. In the circular driveway was a well-used Jeep, next to which Samuels parked the Ford.

What a place, Samuels thought. Terrific place to retire, so quiet." Just the rushing of the river, white water foaming over glistening rocks. And the breeze, it was a hushed presence, at least for the moment, just strong enough to play among the trees, causing even the heaviest limbs to sway in the sky, a canopy of greens and browns, seemingly always in motion. And the smells, pungent and earthy. All and all, a piece of God's half-acre.

"Hi there. Glad you found the old place."

Standing in the doorway was a tall, rather slender man in his mid 50's. He had an athletic build and gave off a kind of nervous activity, even when he was standing still. A pencil-thin mustache embraced his lip, while wire-rimmed glasses shackled his ears. His jet-black hair was slicked back from his hawk-like face, which seemed to see everything in a glance.

"Sol Schwimmer... And you're?

"Robert Samuels."

"From the *San Francisco Chronicle*?"

"Yes."

"Well, grab your things and come on in, Mr. Samuels."

Inside the cabin, which was one large room, Samuels was impressed by the many paintings, mostly natural scenes, hanging from the walls, and an even larger number of black and white photographs competing for space. Two well-worn black leather chairs, and an equally tired couch piled high with books, anchored themselves to the floor. A long, but narrow redwood coffee table added to the sparse décor.

"Sleeping and living quarters below. My studio is above. Makes for a convenient division of labor, don't you think?"

"I could never get away with it in my home," Samuels responded.

"Married?"

"Indeed."

"Well, I'm not."

At his host's urging, Samuels flopped into one of the leather chairs before saying, "Thanks for seeing me."

"I must admit I'm curious as hell. First there was a phone cal from a big wig in Washington, and later your call. That peaked my interest."

"Mr. Schwimmer, I..."

"Call me Sol."

"Sol, I'm here to talk about a stamp."

"Not just any stamp, I take it."

"Quite right."

"And you're doing a story for your paper?"

"Yes."

"So why is Washington interested?"

"I've been asked to write a book."

"About a stamp?"

"And four chaplains."

Sol looked at Samuels for the longest time before he raised himself from the couch. "I'll be damned. So that's it. The government wants to know about the first stamp. It's about time."

"The first stamp?" Samuels said none too calmly. "What first stamp?"

"I'll be right back," Sol said. He disappeared into his upstairs studio, where he pushed and pulled boxes and canvases before exclaiming. "Here it is." He returned with his find and with a flourish propped a large poster board against the coffee table to face Samuels, who now peered at an enlarged photograph, some 2 X 3 feet displaying a postage stamp.

Samuels' face mirrored his feelings, first, elation and excitement, then absolute confusion. Here was an original photograph of the famous stamp. But something was wrong.

"Is there a problem, Mr. Samuels?"

"The faces. There's something different."

"Anything else?"

"The ship, the *Dorchester*… I can't put my finger on it."

"Keep looking."

"The words…"

"What about them?"

"Something been changed."

Sol gave a hearty laugh and slapped his hands together. "Mr. Samuels, you have the makings of a good detective. You're looking at the first stamp, not the second stamp that was eventually printed by the Postal Service. I guess that's what an investigative reporter is when you think about it, a sleuth with a pen."

"I like the analogy."

"Permit me to tell you a story about my father, Mr. Samuels."

My father was Louis Schwimmer. For thirty years he was the head of the art department of the New York branch of the United States Post Office. Bet you didn't know the USPO had an art department, right, Mr. Samuels?"

"Never would have guessed it, Sol."

"Someone has to design all those stamps. Now, as to my dad... Albert Goldman was appointed my father to this position. This was in the 1930's. Goldman was a real promoter. He loved any activity or stunt that brought good publicity to the New York City Post Office, Since my father excelled at making posters, campaign displays, or drawing stamps, he was Goldman's fair-haired kid."

"Always good to be a favorite of the boss."

"Right. In 1948 Goldman met Mrs. Claire A. Wolff. She represented a number of interfaith organizations. They wanted the Post Office to issue a stamp honoring the Four Chaplains. Her request, though heartfelt, was a little unusual for the Post Office. At that time, customarily the Post Office only printed a stamp commemorating someone after the person was dead for ten years. That was the policy. The Immortal Chaplains had only been dead for five years. Goldman, however, realized that such a stamp would be good for business, if you will, and requested a waiver from Washington. It was given."

"Bureaucratic mountains can be moved when the will is there, Sol."

"My father was given the assignment. It was one he delighted in from all I can tell. He had an opportunity to commemorate a fellow Jew, Rabbi Goode, who was one of the Four Chaplains. Historically speaking, this was the first time a Jew was honored by the Post Office. And my father would do it. He poured himself into the work. Using pen and India ink, he made a hand drawing, 7 inches by 12 inches, which included the serrated edges of the final stamp. A lithograph plate was made of his design and sent to Washington for approval. And that's when the fun started.

"Fun?" Samuels asked.

"Politics."

"You will elaborate, I'm sure."

Instead of elaborating, Sol went over to a pile of books, scanned through them, and pulled out a large, green binder, which he handed to Samuels.

"Check this," he said. "Turn to where the book mark shows."

"This will explain everything?" Samuels asked.

"It will help."

Samuels opened the binder and realized immediately what he was looking at. It was a stamp album. Turning to the book marked page, his eyes fell upon one stamp among many, the Four Immortal Chaplains. Samuels glanced at the stamp, then at the larger poster board photograph. Realization came slowly.

"I'm beginning to understand."

～

"A committee in Washington, charged with approving my father's drawing, made a number of revisions. Where the words" Catholic, Protestant, and Jew" had been on his original drawing, they were deleted in order to avoid controversy. No specific religion would be mentioned. Also stricken were the words, "Died to Save Men of All Faiths." No explanation was given for this deletion. Had he known about this and other changes, my father would have been greatly distressed, but he was out of the loop. Others were now making the crucial artistic and editorial decisions. My dad believed the chaplains had participated in a communal act of bravery, that by their sacrifice they had provided us with an extraordinary example of interfaith courage. He believed they were remarkable men and that we should perpetuate their memory. We should honor them. He hoped his rending of their sacrifice, as initially drawn, would do so."

"Somewhat like a movie script, Sol. You hand over your masterpiece to Hollywood and then the studios improve it for the big screen and the directors vision."

"If so, Mr. Samuels, Hollywood was alive and well in Washington. Other revisions were made. My father had drawn the chaplains as men in their mid-50's. This was altered to make them appear in their late

20's. Actually, three were in their 30's and one in his 40's. The ship was redrawn to appear less like a warship and more like an ocean liner."

"And the words?"

They were altered to read, Interfaith in Action. That was okay with my father. The new words were at the heart of the matter. Action had been taken by the chaplains to save lives. They had transcended the exclusiveness of their personal religious belief. You might say that faith conquered theology."

Samuels was listening, even as he gazed intently at the two stamps. The first stamp, unrevised, had it merits, as did the final stamp approved by the Postal Commission. Had he been asked to choose between them, he knew in his heart the revised drawing would receive his vote. Fortunately, Sol did question him on that point.

"That's quite a story, Sol."

"Isn't it?"

"Perhaps I could ask you a question."

"Only one? Be my guest."

"Was there anything in your father's notes about a possible fifth man?"

"Another chaplain?"

"Possibly."

Before answering, Sol gave Samuels a sharp look, as if he was trying to fathom the reporter's inner soul. He surprised Samuels with his response.

"Mr. Samuels, do you think," he said, "you could have done what the Chaplains did?"

"No. I'm no hero. I learned that off Okinawa in '45."

"You were on the *Aaron Ward*?"

"How did you know?"

"I skimmed through your book, *Miracle at RPS 10* in preparation for our meeting."

"I'm flattered. But now you know. I lacked heroic status."

"But you are a brave man. Who knows what you would do if pushed to the limit."

Samuels let the words hang. What could he say? And where, he thought, was this going?

"Mr. Samuels, a question. You know my father was an Orthodox Jew. He believed very strongly in a compassionate, merciful God. Do you believe in such a God?"

Samuels was taken aback by the question. He wanted to know about a possible "fifth chaplain." He didn't want to probe metaphysical questions. He was also troubled that he was now on the stick end of challenging questions.

"Yes, I suppose I do," Samuels answered reluctantly.

"With fervor?"

"Yes, but that was when eight kamikaze planes were crashing into the Aaron *Ward*."

"And you thought you were going to die?"

"When I wanted to live."

"And now?"

"I have, if possible, the fervor of an agnostic."

"You do not believe in a personal God, Mr. Samuels?"

"One interested in my daily doings, no."

"But you still wanted God to save you?"

"Yes. I see where you're going. Yes, I wanted God, if such a deity existed, to take a personal interest in me. I wanted to survive."

"Understandable."

For a moment, silence prevailed. Neither man spoke. For his part, Samuels found himself challenged by his own thoughts. The last kamikaze plane had barely missed the *Ward*, exploding scant yards from the ship's bridge before crashing into the sea. Had the physics of guns, distance, and angle downed the Jap, or had God taken a hand in the affairs of man? Was it the skill of the gunners, which downed the plane, or was a larger divine plan at work? Had the USA deity defeated the Emperor's god? Too many questions and two few answers, at least at this moment. His mental gyrations notwithstanding, he needed time out from these probing inquires.

"A fifth chaplain, Sol?"

"Mr. Samuels, my father spoke to a man who survived the *Dorchester's* disaster. He wanted to learn what happened that night, to incorporate the emotions of that man and others into his stamp design. That man lives in Brooklyn. His name is Ben Epstein. You should see him. He, I hope, will be able to assist you."

"He spoke to your father about a 'fifth man?'"

"They spoke about many things."

Samuels paused to consider a last question, which demanded an answer. "Why the questions about God?"

"Oh, Mr. Samuels, before your quest is completed, I think you will answer that question on your own. Somehow, there is a connection, I believe, between the two ships, the *Aaron Ward* and the *Dorchester,* united by your quest to find spiritual meaning in the presence of dreadful violence. For you, Okinawa and the North Atlantic are the same moment; they are not separated by time and distance. On some level, it appears to me, you're seeking to reconcile the pain of surviving, while so many others died.

http://www.schwimmer.com/fourchaplains/

CHAPTER 8

UPDATES

FEBRUARY 1962 – NORTHERN CALIFORNIA

REPORT TO KURTZ FROM SAMUELS

As per your recommendation, I met with Sol Schwimmer in Weaverville, California. Nice town. Beautiful country. Great fishing from what I hear.

The focus of our discussion was the first Four Chaplains stamp, which was drawn by his father, Louis Schwimmer. This was done at the urging of the New York Postmaster, Albert Goldman. We also reviewed the changes made in Washington, which resulted in a different stamp eventually printed by the Post Office.

At no time did the son, based on his discussions with his father, indicate any knowledge of a "fifth man." On the other, he didn't discount the possibility.

He did, however, suggest that I see a Mr. Ben Epstein, who lives in Brooklyn, New York. Apparently, Epstein, a survivor of the *Dorchester* tragedy, spoke with the father and was an eyewitness to the ship's last minutes. I intend to visit Epstein next week. I'm taking TWA flight 1492 to La Guardia.

Further updates will follow.

Samuels

RESPONSE

A White House courier will meet you with a complete background report on Epstein.

Kurtz

REPORT TO HOOVER FROM BRADY AND HILL

As directed, we followed the subject to Weaverville, where he met with Sol Schwimmer. Again, as authorized, an agent from San Francisco office placed a "bug" in Schwimmer's home before he met with Samuels. A complete transcript of their meeting is attached.

Two things stand out. First, Samuels is searching for a "fifth chaplain." Second, he plans to see a Ben Epstein in Brooklyn, who may know something about this. He is booked on TWA flight 1492, as are we.

Brady and Hill

RESPONSE

Maintain contact with subject. Provide daily reports.

Hoover

REPORT TO STRETCH FROM NAILS AND BALDY

We followed the reporter to Weaverville, California, and to the home of Sol Schwimmer. We were unable to determine what they discussed. Samuels drove back to San Francisco the next day.

Two points: we think the FBI or some other agency is keeping tabs on Samuels, as an unmarked vehicle followed him. Also, this appears to be some type of Jewish conspiracy, since Kurtz, Schwimmer, and Samuels are all Jews.

Request instructions.

Nails and Baldy

RESPONSE

My "source" believes the FBI is shadowing Samuels. The purpose of his visit was to gain information about a "fifth chaplain." Samuels is headed for Brooklyn, New York, TWA flight 1492. Follow him there. A Klan member will meet you at the airport.

Stretch

ROBERT KENNEDY'S REPORT TO THE PRESIDENT

As hoped, Samuels is a competent researcher hot on the trail or the illusive "fifth chaplain." The FBI is watching his back. There is some indication that the KKK is on to our effort. Kurtz is providing information as necessary. Stay safe.

RK

CHAPTER 9

THE SOURCE

FEBRUARY 1962 – THE WHITE HOUSE

Each morning three men met with the Vice-President of the United States, Lyndon B. Johnson. They provided the V.P. with the latest information concerning possible domestic violence. Ordinarily, their updates fell into three categories: civil rights demonstrations, especially in the Deep South; anti-war marches concerning the nation's southeast Asian foreign policy; and college sit-in's, whether to protest a law, or to labor on behalf of a group, such as the poor.

The committee worked within the Justice Department and reported directly to the Attorney-General, Robert Kennedy, before prepping the Vice-President. Members of the committee had impeccable backgrounds and the highest possible security clearances. All were domestic violence experts with years of experience in the field, either with the FBI, state law enforcement, or the military. They were the "best of the best" and the White House depended on their daily impartial and highly rational analysis of potential threats. All were men with an intense love of the country with an unquestioned loyalty to it.

But one of them was a spy.

The Source didn't look like a spy. Physically, he was best described as "Mr. Average," an average guy in everyway, slight of build, middle age, and balding. People thought of him as a quiet guy, even shy, certainly not as an "out-in-front" leader. As a committee member, he was a listener, not a talker. When he spoke, he was low-keyed and sparse with his words. His colleagues respected his input as focused, well thought out, and highly accurate in predicting events. In short, he was a valuable member of the team.

He was also a member of the KKK.

The Source was an academic before joining the Justice Department. He had made his name at the University of Tennessee in its Department of Criminology, where he was a renowned lecturer and researcher. Two books had put him on the map, so to speak. The first, The *History of Dissent in America*, was a ponderous effort to detail dissent from the Puritans through the McCarthy period. Though not a best seller with the Book-of-the-Month Club, it was a widely used text on college campuses. His second book entitled, *New Wave Challenges*, focused on the Civil Rights movement and anti-war protests. It was this effort, which brought him to the attention of the Justice Department.

If it was possible to be a moderate member of the KKK, the Source was such a person. He was opposed to extra-legal activities, especially physical violence against Negroes, including, of course, lynchings. He considered physical intimidation counter-productive. Rather, he supported and hoped to maintain de jure laws in all their racial forms throughout the South, that is, the system of segregation based on Jim Crow laws. Given that, he supported the Plessey v. Ferguson decision (1890) to maintain into the future "separate but equal facilities, most importantly in the schools and housing."

Separation of the races in these matters was important to him, as it was to northerners based on de facto segregation patterns beyond the famous Mason-Dixon line. The difference between Chicago's Negro ghetto and one found in Atlanta or New Orleans was only a matter of customs and law, and possibly in degree.

He was not opposed to suffrage; the Negro had and should use the vote to advocate for issues important to him. He was not opposed to providing the Negro with first rate schools, housing, and jobs. He simply opposed the forced integration of races pushed by social planners in Washington. In his reasoning, the races could flourish without being forced upon one another by law, or federal troops. Quite surprisingly, he saw himself as a non-violent advocate of KKK views, almost in the manner of Martin L. King, who supported civil disobedience along the lines of Gandhi and Thoreau.

The Source was well aware of the President's desire to propose new civil rights legislation to Congress in 1963. He was also privy to Kurtz's effort to have Robert Samuels research the "fifth man" idea. He knew the "what" and the "why" of this effort, and was quietly opposing it. He was fully aware of Hoover's operatives, Hill and Brady.

It paid, the Source knew, to be on the inside, a trusted member of the government, who reported to Robert Kennedy' s Justice Department on a daily basis. Even if he wanted to, the Source couldn't have conceived of a better situation.

CHAPTER 10

THE SURVIVOR

LATE FEBRUARY 1962 – BROOKLYN, NEW YORK CITY

True to his word, Kurtz had a courier meet Robert Samuels at La Guardia Airport.

"This package is for you, Mr. Samuels. Also, you've been booked into the Astoria Hotel for three nights. I recommend that you use cabs rather than drive yourself. This town can be a bear for visitors."

"The information about Ben Epstein?"

"What we have, inside."

"Any other words of encouragement?"

"We believe you being followed?"

"By whom?"

"We're working on that."

"In Weaverville?"

"We think so."

Samuels thought about that for a moment. His next question was, of course, predictable.

"Do I need to take any precautions?"

"Just do your research."

"Will Kurtz have anyone watching my back?"

The courier smiled and shrugged. In response, Samuels did the same. What else could he do, he asked himself? Not much was generally the answer. It was like at Okinawa. You stood watch aboard the destroyer hoping the kamikazes wouldn't show and knowing full well they would. Would your ship catch it? Would his ship bear the brunt of the attack? You were there to protect the big ships, especially the aircraft carriers. But who was there to protect you? The truth was you were on your own, as it was in his hunt to track down, if possible, the "fifth chaplain."

After leaving Weaverville, Samuels had spent three days at home catching up on his personal life, how the kids were doing, paying bills, and romancing his wife. The kids were fine. Rachel had a new love in her life and excellent grades in school. Matt was pitching better than ever and doing his homework. Kieran seemed to be flourishing in his new school and was fitting well into his adopted but temporary family. Apparently, he had tried out for the cross-country team and made the junior varsity squad quite to the delight of all.

Before giving in to his romantic inclinations, Lynn had transcribed his notes from the meeting with Sol Schwimmer.

"What a story," she exclaimed.

"Isn't it?"

"Two stamps… A story" within a story…

"Lynn, that was my feeling, too."

"Can you get it into the *Chronicle*?"

"I'm writing up a human interest feature right now, which focuses on the stamps."

"Will Kurtz be upset?"

"I don't think so. I never mention what I'm really researching. You know, the fifth man.'"

"Do you think there was a another chaplain?'

"There's no evidence to suggest so at this time, but…"

"Yes?"

"This guy I'm meeting in Brooklyn, Ben Epstein… Who knows? Maybe he'll shed some light."

"Would you like it to be true?"

Samuels thought about Lynn's question. The Four Chaplains were called the "immortal chaplains" at this time. Would the existence of a fifth chaplain change all that? If the fifth person were indeed a Negro, what would the public's response be? If he existed, would Kennedy's legislation be helped or hurt by the disclosure?

"Yes. I want it to be true."

The drive to the Astoria from the airport took about one hour. As the cab worked its way through the city's legendary traffic, Samuels tried to remember what he knew about Brooklyn besides the Dodgers, who had left the confines of Flatbush for Los Angeles' greener revenue.

He knew it was the most populous borough with over 2 million residents. It also had the greatest population density of any county in the United States. He was aware that Brooklyn prided itself on its own, independent neighborhood cultures made up of different ethnic groups. It was also part of Long Island due to its Dutch history. He had read somewhere that Brooklyn came from Brookland, which was derived from the Dutch Breuckelen. Just some trivia to keep the brain cells as alert as possible.

As they approached the borough, the Yellow Cab crossed over the famous Brooklyn Bridge, which, when completed in the previous century, ended the need for a ferryboat ride to Manhattan. A few years later, Brooklyn's residents voted by a slight majority to join with Manhattan, the Bronx, Queens, and Staten Island to become the five boroughs of the modern New York city.

That night, Samuels read and reread the precious little information the government had about Ben Epstein. He was an Army private who trained at Camp Miles Standish before embarking on the *Dorchester*. He had survived the German torpedo, his injuries, and the war. He lived in Brooklyn, where he was an accountant with an interest in the furniture business. He was married to Miriam Burg. They had two kids. Until recently, he seldom talked about his lonely plunge into the freezing Atlantic moments before the *Dorchester* slid into the abyss, disappearing forever into the past.

Samuels thought about how he would approach Epstein. Should he just come out and ask, "Look, was there a 'fifth chaplain' on the ship?" Or would it be better to simply let Epstein tell his story and lead up to the question? Samuels decided on the latter. Sometimes it's just better to go with the flow.

The next day Samuels took a cab to Epstein's home, a nice three-bedroom cottage smack in the middle of Flatbush. A short balding man met him at the front door. He offered a vigorous handshake and a radiant smile.

"Mr. Samuels, at last. Been expecting you since your call. Come on in."

"I appreciate your cooperation, Mr. Epstein."

"Call me Ben."

"Of course."

Epstein escorted Samuels to the living room, which was decorated with floral wallpaper, highly polished New England maple furniture, and numerous family pictures on mantles, a hutch, and coffee table. Samuels found himself looking at one picture in particular, which showed a younger Ben Epstein in his Army uniform smiling at the camera.

"That was 1943. Just before we left Camp Miles Standish. Just before we boarded the *Dorchester.*"

"January 22, 1943?"

"You've done your homework."

Evading the question, Samuels asked, "Your family, they're not at home today?"

"Sent my wife packing to her sister for the day. I wanted us to have a private conversation."

"Private…?"

"I don't enjoy talking about the *Dorchester*. Bad memories. You understand, don't you?"

"Very much so. I brought a few back from the Pacific myself."

"Well, then let's get to it, Mr. Samuels. You're writing a book, I understand. What do you want to know?"

"Whatever comes to your mind."

"It was January 22, 1943, when I arrived at Pier II on Staten Island. That's when I first saw the *Dorchester*, all 367 feet of her, all 5,680 tons of her. I had never seen a ship so large. It was raining. I recall that and it was cold. I was soaked standing in line waiting for my name to be called. I was one of over 500 Army guys embarking that morning.

"That when you first saw the chaplains?"

"Right. They were greeting each man once he boarded. You know, just getting acquainted and sharing some advice, or pointing out when services would take place. The usual stuff you'd expect of chaplains."

"Did you know your destination? Did they?"

"No. Some of us thought we were going to North Africa. A few smart guys figured we were going to Iceland because of all the warm weather gear stored aboard the ship. But really, we had no idea we were headed for a highly secret base in Greenland, no idea at all."

"Would it have made any difference?"

"None. We were in the hands of God and the US Army."

"The trip over… How was it?"

"My bunk was three stories down in the hold of the ship along with a lot of other guys. What a place that was! Most of us had never been to sea before and before long old mother sea sickness hit us. It was a terrible trip. I was as sick as a dog. I just lay and bed and moaned. I was no John Wayne superhero. This was no cruise to the Caribbean."

"You drilled aboard ship?"

"Did we. Sick or not, they made us conduct emergency drills, almost every day. I was coupled with a buddy, Vincent Frucelli, and we practiced abandoning ship drills. We were taught to reach the upper deck and inflate doughnut rafts, which we then threw into the sea. After that, we were supposed to jump into the water and swim to one of them. However, no one said anything doing it at night after a torpedo blew a truck-size hole in our side. They didn't say anything about the water, but we knew. With a water temperature of 35 degrees, a guy could last maybe twenty minutes. Still, we drilled and I'm glad we did. Saved my life."

"Saved others, too."

"Not enough. Now let's get back to the drilling aboard ship for a moment, okay. Mr. Samuels? The Navy loved the concept. Drill. Repeat drill. Do it once more. Faster. More proficient. Men hated it. Men loved it when it saved their lives. It must have been that way on the *Aaron Ward*. Drilling each day. Fire control drills… Gun drills… Emergency medical drills… And it paid off when the Jap planes dove on you, determined to die by crashing into us. And other men, this time in the air, seeking a glorious death in the name of their Emperor by immolating themselves on our ship's deck."

"We were told, Mr. Samuels, to sleep in our heavy clothing and to keep our shoes on. The Captain required everyone to wear his life preserver even in the sack. If you had gloves, you were asked to keep them on you. Every night in that stinging hot hole, I slept that way. Very uncomfortable, I can tell you. A lot of guys didn't. When the torpedo hit some of them never had time to find their shoes."

"The Captain was a smart man, Ben."

"You bet. After we left St. Johns, Newfoundland, the Captain knew we were being shadowed by German U-boats. At 8 to 10 knots, we were a sitting duck. He prepared us as best he could."

"What happened?"

"There was a loud explosion sometime after midnight. I knew right away the ship was in trouble. Don't ask me how. Some survival instinct maybe; I don't know. I climbed to the main deck with Vincent. As trained, we threw a doughnut raft into the water. I told my buddy to climb down a rope after me and then to jump into the sea. Then swim for anything afloat. I did this, but he didn't. I never saw him go into the water. I never saw him again. I liked that guy. I think about him every day.

"The water was damn cold, shockingly. It took your breath away. It was like jumping into a pitcher of ice cubes. After the war, I used to wake up in a panic, shivering and shaking all over, reliving that damn moment. Sometimes I'd just jump into the shower just to stand under the hot water for five minutes with my eyes closed. Used to scare the daylights out of the wife."

"You made it to safety, did you not?"

"I did, but it wasn't easy. Oil from the ship was everywhere. It was in my ears, eyes, all over my clothes. Ugly stuff. But it probably saved my life. It acted as a kind of insulation to keep out the cold. I was a strong swimmer, but in the dark I couldn't find a life raft or boat. I figured I was going to die. I was so cold, so frightened, so darn wet. In my head, I saw pictures of my family, my mother and father, and my brothers. I even saw Vince's face. I guess I was beginning to hallucinate. I'm told that happens."

"But you didn't give up hope?"

"It looked like the end for me. At that point, I was ready to die. I had decided I could live with that."

"You were ready to die?"

"Not much else I could do. You must have had that feeling in the Pacific."

Samuels mind clicked on the last kamikaze plane heading toward the *Ward*, seemingly coming directly at him, as if he had a large bulls eye on his chest. In that moment, he thought he was going to die. Curiously, he wasn't scared. That would come later. It was as if he found a degree of peace in accepting the fact. He had done his duty. In a moment it would be over. End of Robert Samuels... End of story...

"I remember, Ben. That 'Zero!' It had my name on it, I swear to you. I just watched the Jap pilot glide in through the 20mm gun screen. Nothing, it seemed, could stop it."

"But something did."

"A kid, hardly eighteen years old, kept firing away with his 20mm gun."

"And?"

"The plane blew up right in my face."

"It was a miracle?"

Samuels didn't like the term miracle, even though he had used the word in the titles of his two books. It suggested metaphysical factors beyond his under-standing, the involvement of a greater deity, or the acting out of some grand plan, which he could not comprehend. Was it the physics, he had asked himself a hundred times, or the kid's bullets arching their way through the geometry of death, or the hand of God sweeping over the *Ward* that day so long ago? Samuels had never resolved this question.

"Ben, something happened."

"I know."

~

"I was swimming in the black water in the black night trying to find anything I could grab onto. In those last moments I had faith I'd make it. I come from a people who have had to overcome every mountain, every horror, every tyrant, every evil, and they always did because they had faith. I had faith that night.

"Suddenly, I saw a lifeboat, one of two out of fourteen boats, which had been successfully launched. I headed toward it. The boat was already full. Nobody wanted another water-soaked person aboard who might capsize it. I reached the boat, but I couldn't get my leg over the side. It was frozen. Just when I thought I had had it, two men reached down and dragged me into the boat."

"Unbelievable."

"I never knew who they were. I didn't know if they survived

68

the night. I owed them my life. Maybe they were angels dressed in soaked blues. This I do know. They risked their lives to save me."

"It sounds like there were a lot of chaplains at work that night, aboard the *Dorchester* and in the water."

"Perhaps. I choose that moment to gaze back at the *Dorchester*. Don't ask me why. No good reason. Just happened. The old ship was making her last lurching movement into the water. She rolled to starboard stern first and slowly descended into the sea. I was told later, it was exactly 1:20 a.m., or 25-minutes after she had been attacked. I saw hundreds of men clinging to her railings, going down with the ship instead of jumping into the sea. They seemed too terrified to let go of the railing. I couldn't understand why they didn't jump. Just jump you dumb bastards. It was the most horrible thing I've ever seen. I'll never get that scene out of my mind."

"Did you see the Four Chaplains, Ben?"

"No, not at the end."

"When?"

"When I first got to the main deck. I saw them in a large group. They were speaking calmly and quietly to the men, trying to allay their fears. They were handing out life jackets and gloves."

"Just the four of them?"

"Well, I think Big Hit was there, too.

"Who?"

"Big Hit, he was our chief cook, a former prize fighter."

"What was he doing exactly?"

"He was helping the Chaplains. You know, passing out life jackets."

"What happened to him?"

"Don't know… I never saw him again."

"Funny about that sort of thing … I saw a kid on the *Ward* firing away, just a teen barely out of high school. Then the explosion… The fire… The smoke… The smell of death… The pounding in the ears… The blast of heat… The shrapnel whizzing by my ears… The yelling… The cry, "Medic! Medic! Sounds and smells overlapping each other… And then the realization… I'm alive. Then the need to see my savior… I looked around. Where was the kid? Where?"

"Please, continue, Ben."

"I was in the boat for almost an hour before help came. Guys were freezing to death all around me and in the water. At first, we thought it was the German sub, which had torpedoed us. But it was the Coast Guard Cutter, *Escanaba*. The cutter closed in on us and told us to jump onto a cargo net hanging from its deck. You could only do this when a wave carried you to the highest point next to the cutter. It was a tough jump with the sun out and no drift between the lifeboats and the *Dorchester*. If you misjudged, you could be crushed between the lifeboat and the ship. I couldn't do it. I was near frozen. Now I figured I was going to die in sight of salvation. I had to admit, my faith was beginning to slacken. Then, a miracle happened. Two sailors from the cutter climbed down the cargo net and carried me, a near frozen lump, back up onto their ship."

"Luck was with you that night, Ben."

"I guess so."

"Ever find out who these guys were?"

"Just members of the crew, I think. One was an officer, the other was a mess cook, I was told later. All I know is this. They were angels who appeared out of the night at the last possible second. I never knew. Did they survive the war? Never found out. Did they risk their lives to save other? I assume so."

"What happened next?"

"I was taken immediately to a galley below deck and placed on a damn hard table. A doctor, Dr. Ralph Nix, ordered my clothes cut off my body. Five men were assigned to rub me, two for my arms, two for my legs and feet, and one for my torso. Those guys rubbed. Hell, they almost rubbed off my skin. The doctor poured alcohol down my throat, but I couldn't feel it. Finally, about when those guys could hardly rub more, I began to feel sensation in my feet.

The doctor grabbed me and hugged me, and I sure some of those tough sailors were crying. I know I was. Afterwards, I was placed in a bunk below another fellow who had been fished out of the sea. We weren't permitted to go to sleep. We had to stay awake to stay alive by maintaining some movement. I was order to kick the bottom of his bed, while another guy to that to mine. I kicked all night. Used to wake up doing that. Scared the dickens out of my wife. Then I cry. Nice to have a good wife at times like that.

"You made it, Ben."

"You made it, too, Mr. Samuels."

"Yeah."

I remembered. I couldn't find the kid at first. Too much confusion… Then I saw him face down on the deck, blood seeping from his fatal wounds. Just a kid… Probably lied about his age to join up. Some farmer's boy, most probably, freckle-faced, and sprawled on the deck, dead. My life, saved by a miracle, but at such a price.

"Just a matter of faith, Mr. Samuels?"

"You think so?"

"I know so, and you do, too."

The two men were quiet now. They needed a moment to collect their thoughts. Ben finally spoke.

"Could you have done it, Mr. Samuels?"

"What, Ben?"

"Could you have given your life jacket to someone else?"

"Like the Chaplains?"

"Yes, like them."

"I don't think so. That's heroism beyond belief, that's a bravery beyond my understanding."

"My thinking, too. Absolutely, I couldn't do what they did."

"That's why they're the Immortal Chaplains."

"That's why they should be remembered, Mr. Samuels. They had faith. Tell the world about them in your book. Keep them alive."

As Samuels left Ben's home later, he made a silent pledge to "the man in the water." The Immortal Chaplains would not die, and, if there was a Fifth Chaplain, Samuels would find him.

CHAPTER 11

THE CRUEL DECISION

EARLY MARCH – 1962 – SAN FRANCISCO

Robert Samuels was back home. He needed to be home. He was dead tired from traveling across the country. But more than that, he was still dealing with Ben Epstein's story and the survivor's probing questions about Samuel's faith. As a reporter, he was supposed to ask the questions, elicit information, and hunt for the elusive commodity called truth. Things, however, had been turned upside down in Brooklyn, as in Weaverville. Ben Epstein like Sol Schwimmer had pushed him in ways he had not expected. Sol had wanted to know if he believed in God. Ben had narrowed the question to one of faith. But faith in what, he wondered?? God? Man? Should he believe in the randomness of the universe or some grand plan beyond his limited comprehension? In doing so, each man had confronted him with theological questions concerning his core beliefs.

What did he believe? Though raised as a Jew, did Samuels truly believe in a God lurking behind his agnostic wall of doubt? Did he have faith to carry him where rationality and empirical observation refused to go? Sol and Ben, unlike Samuels, seemed to have made some great leap of faith. For them, there was a God who intervened in the affairs of men. Sol believed that randomness alone was not an explanation for Louis Schwimmer's involvement with the stamp honoring the Four Immortal Chaplains. Ben wouldn't accept the fickleness of chance to account for his survival in a sea of death. And, as they both hinted, statistical probability alone did not reveal why Robert Samuels was on a quest seeking a "Fifth Chaplain."

What did Robert Samuels really believe? The question refused to disappear. It hung around like a bad cold. Sol had said... No he had hinted Samuels would find God as he pursued his research. Not only that, but that he would need God to complete this task. Ben believed Samuels had more faith than he was willing to admit, as when doubt was overcome in the moment the last kamikaze exploded mere yards from him.

Samuels found himself unable to get beyond their insights, or perhaps more precisely, their accusations. At the heart of the matter, one question swirled in his mind: beyond being a married reporter with three kids in his house, who was Robert Samuels in the great scheme of things? The query tugged at him.

Once he was home Samuels had shared Ben's story with his wife and the kids, but not the question troubling him. They, as had he, were impressed by Ben's narrative.

"Dad, it really happened?" Matt asked.

"Absolutely."

"All those men in the water, freezing," Lynn said with emotion cracking her voice.

"Why did it take so long for the coast guard ships to rescue them?" Rachel asked with a tinge of anger in her voice. "More people should have been saved."

"You mentioned 'red lights' on the life jackets, Dad," Matt stated, "what were they for? Was it a way to locate someone in the water?"

"The captains of the surviving ships must have known the men couldn't last long in freezing water," Kieran declared harshly.

It's nice having smart kids. They may bug you with the "why's" of life, or the "how come's," but they do ask good questions. Not to be outdone by the youthful crowd, Lynn asked, "Why was the ship going to Greenland anyway?"

"Good questions. Let's take them one at a time. What I'm going to tell you comes from the Navy's Official Records and it's only for you guys. Okay?"

RESCUE AT SEA – CRUEL DECISION

The *Dorchester* was within 150 miles of the Greenland coast when the *U-223*, the German submarine, fired three torpedoes at the troopship. The *Dorchester* was part of convoy SG-19 composed six ships. The command ship, the *Tampa*, was 3,000 yards in front of two merchant ships troopships, the *Lutz*, the *Biscaya*, and the troop-ship, *Dorchester*. Two pre-war Coast Guard cutters straddled the convoy, the *Escanaba* and the *Comanche*. As a group, the ships, now tightly close to each other, steamed through stormy seas and an almost moonless night at a modest eight knots. The ships, however, had not been ordered to follow a zig-zag pattern through waters infested with German "wolf packs," thereby making them a more elusive target.

It was February 3, 1943, a little before midnight. All was calm on the surface.

The *Tampa* was the senior ship in the convoy. The convoy commander, Captain Joseph Greenspun was aboard the Tampa. All orders concerning speed, course, and formation came from the *Tampa*. No radio communication was permitted. All communication was by signal lamp.

After the *U-223* successfully torpedoed the *Dorchester*, Captain Greenspun ordered the *Escanaba* and *Comanche* to hunt for the submarine. The *Tampa* would shelter the two merchant ships to Greenland. This questionable decision doomed the men in the icy water. Captain Greenspun put aside humanitarian considerations. He wanted to destroy the German submarine before it attacked one of his merchant ships. In doing so, he was following the unwritten policy of the Navy. His first priority did not include the *Dorchester's* crew.

It wasn't until 1:43 a.m., about 48 minutes after the explosion that the order was given to rescue survivors. By then, it was too late for the men in the water. For many, Captain Greenspun's decision was morally reprehensible.

"How could he do that?" Rachel asked, almost screaming at her father. "He just let those men die."

"He should have been thrown out of the Navy," Matt said with real anger in his voice. "Or put into the brig forever."

"Or made to walk the plank," Kieran added. "Pirate justice for him."

"Dear God," Lynn said, almost tearfully.

What could Samuels say? His family felt the same revulsion he experienced when he first read the Navy's Official Report. And then the anger set in when he learned the *U-223* was beneath the surface, some 500 feet down, fearful of depth charges. Rather than attacking another ship in the convoy, the sub was cowering in anticipation of a depth charge attack. There had never been any need for the cutters to go after her. Men had died for no good reason.

Samuels decided to keep this information to himself. There would be time later to share it.

"Did I tell you about the rescue swimmers?" Samuels asked.

"No," Matt said abruptly. "What about them?"

"On both Coast Guard Cutters, specially trained men wore rubber suits to ward off the frigid water. With a line attached to them, they jumped into the water to rescue men too weak to climb up the cargo nets, or even to swim to the ships. These retrievers would grab hold of a man, and with the help of a crewman, pull the near dead guy aboard. Almost all the rescued men were suffering from hypothermia and could not climb aboard without assistance. The retrievers went into the water many times that night and were instrumental in helping to save at least ninety-three men. These Coast Guard guys on the *Escanaba* and the *Comanche* were real heroes."

"I should say," Lynn said. "What courage."

"Did any of those men die?" Rachel asked.

"The records indicate that one died from overexposure. He went into the sea once too many times."

"He's a real hero," Matt said.

"The red lights, Dad. What were they for?" asked Matt.

Samuels was almost afraid to tell his family. In some ways, this was the final horror of the sinking.

"The life jackets had a water-activated signal light, which extended above the wearer at the shoulder. The signal light blinked red continuously, whether the man was alive or frozen to death. Hundreds of men were in the water with their signal lights faithfully working. It was at once very beautiful in the cruelest possible way. The blinking lights were supposed to save a man.

The rescuers would see the lights; men would not be lost to the lapping waves. But the Coast Guard cutters didn't come soon enough. Already dead, hundreds of men floated in the oil slick water with their lights still blinking."

"My God," Lynn said. "What a terrible way to die."

"Jesus," Rachel yelped. "I can't believe it."

"Damn," Matt groaned. "Those guys never had a chance."

"The plank's too good for that Captain," Kieran added fiercely.

Watching his family, Samuels was unsure what to say to alleviate the emotional distress they were dealing with on an empathetic level. He, at least, had an opportunity over the past few deals days to square himself with the plight of the *Dorchester's* sinking. Even so, it pained him to think about it. More than that, he felt an unresolved anger. More men should have been saved. More men could have been saved.

"Robert, you're going to write this story for the *Chronicle*?" Lynn asked.

"People need to know about this," Rachel added.

"Do it, Dad," Matt nudged.

"Kieran, your thoughts?"

"Firing squad."

At that moment Robert Samuels decided he would never, if possible, run afoul of this group. They took no prisoners.

"Already written and submitted, Lynn. The story will be in tomorrow's early edition."

"That's my guy. It will make an absolutely great follow up to the stamp story."

Samuels thought about Lynn's comment. He was satisfied with what he had written. He was good at story telling. And he had told this story well. He wondered if it would elicit the many letters to the editor as his first effort. Apparently, he had touched many people for whom the war was still a recent, but sad memory. A few hundred letters, mostly favorable, had poured into the *Chronicle*. And more were coming each day. He had connected with his reading audience.

"Dad," Rachel said, "you said you would tell us about Greenland."

"Right."

Thank god, Samuels thought, they didn't ask me about the lifeboats and the ensuing panic on the *Dorchester*.

Many men were killed almost instantly when the torpedo exploded. Those who survived the initial blast found themselves in the crowded hold of the ship with their exit to the top deck blocked by crates of cola bottles that had fallen into the corridors. Confusion and panic struck immediately, especially when the lights dimmed out and the emergency lights failed to kick in. Others died after inhaling air contaminated with ammonia fumes. A few made it out alive by breathing through handkerchiefs. Most didn't make it out of the hold.

The *Dorchester* had sailed with enough boats and rafts to accommodate 1,286 people in theory. That should have been enough for the 900 people aboard the ship. It should have been under the best of circumstances. There were thirteen lifeboats without motors. There was one boat with a motor. There were forty-five rubber doughnut rafts, and two square wooden rafts kept afloat by an oil drum tied at each end. But not all the rafts and boats were available. No craft could be launched on the starboard side because of damaged caused by the torpedo, which caused the *Dorchester* to roll to that side. This made it impossible to reach life craft. Due to this, the port side was overcrowded with panicky people, who piled into boats in such numbers that the boats capsized.

Still other boats couldn't be lowered because their cables were frozen with encrusted ice. Some boats, once launched, struck the hull of the ship on the way down and dumped the occupants into the sea.

In the confusion wrought by the torpedo explosion at night, most of the men ignored or simply forgot what little they had been taught in their lifeboat drills. Panic. Driven by fear, took over. Men forgot how to get to their assigned boats using a system based on their initials. But who could blame them? The ship was alive with clanging bells, screaming sirens, and the frenzied cries. All of which fed the increasing uncontrollable fear.

The ugliness of the night continued. Many men jumped into the freezing water before the *Dorchester* slowed and stopped, and before lifeboats were launched. In the cold North Atlantic they couldn't catch up to either. They died trying. Hypothermia won. Other men were killed fighting each other as they raced to the lifeboats. Others, half-blinded by smoke and dust, fell into craters created by the torpedo as they clumsily hurried across the deck. Death marched across the *Dorchester's* deck that night.

"Robert, did you hear Rachel's question?"

"He's zoning again," Matt said.

"What's zoning?" Kieran quizzed.

"Dad disappears for a while into himself. Hides out until he ready to deal with reality."

"Really?"

Of course, as might be expected, Samuels chose that moment to reenter the conversation, saying, "Sorry guys. I was thinking of other things. As to Greenland…"

BLUIE WEST ONE –THE SECRET BASE

"Greenland's importance to the United States began in the 1930's. Thinking way ahead, the Navy decided to give every country and/or land area in the world a code name, which could be used in case a war broke out. For example, Aaron was the code name for New Britain, a South Pacific Island. The code name for the Yukon was Zouave. Greenland was given a colorful name, Bluie.

"A few words about Greenland… Lying almost entirely within the Arctic Circle, it's the largest island in the world. Denmark administers the area, as it has since it became a colony in 1815. The small population, composed mainly of Inuit people, resides mostly along the southern coast.

"Greenland was the first European settlement in the New World. Erik the Red explored the island in 983 A.D. At that time, the climate was warmer than today. The area teemed with birds and the sea was excellent for fishing. There were many fjords, where anchorage was good. Enormous meadows existed and there was an abundant supply of grass, willows, junipers, and birch trees. Unfortunately, a thick ice cap covered most of the land. Glaciers on land and icebergs off shore were part of the environment. Keeping this in mind, Erik the Red, who would have been a great land promoter today, called the island Greenland in order to encourage migration. He was quite a salesman. Historians argue he was assisted by a grievous year of famine in 976 A.D., which fell upon northwestern Europe and England. Many people were hungry for food as well as land. Erick the Red could offer both.

"Greenland's importance grew with the onset of World War II. Both Germany and England wanted to control of the island. Denmark, which had been overrun by the Nazis, was in no position to defend its colony. Both London and Berlin had good reasons for wanting Greenland within their sphere of influence. Near Ivigtut, there was a cryolite mine, an ore, which was needed to produce aluminum. Situated astride the North Atlantic shipping lanes, long-range planes could attack merchant ships from an unsinkable aircraft carrier. Meteorologists considered Greenland an ideal location for a weather base.

"And one other thing... For planes flying from America to England, the best route was from Boston to Newfoundland, then across the Atlantic to Iceland and Greenland before flying to Scotland and the British Isles. The reverse was also true if Greenland and Iceland were in German hands.

"After Germany declared war on the United States, Henrik Kauffman, the Danish minister to Washington, signed an agreement to make Greenland an American protectorate for the course of the war. Code named Bluie, Greenland fast became an important outpost in America's military strategy. To control Greenland was to control the North Atlantic.

"In late 1942, the McKinley Dredging Company was contracted to build a 5,000-foot long airfield on a glacial moraine near the town Narsarsuaq. Surrounded by nearby mountains, landing planes had to fly 52-miles up Eriksfjord at low elevation. More than 10,000 aircraft made this dangerous approach during the war on route to England or North Africa. Greenland became, under American control, a defensible air station in the middle of the North Atlantic, and a thorn in the side of Nazi Germany.

"The air base and the military installations, which served it, were known as Bluie West 1. The *Dorchester* and the two merchant ships in the convoy were carrying construction supplies, civilian workers, scientists, and military personnel to protect the base from any German effort to take over the island. The *Dorchester's* mission was important, secret, and ultimately tragic."

"That's a great story, Mr. Samuels."
"Thanks, Kieran."

"Wow," Matt volunteered. "I never learned anything like that in school."

"Dad, will you write about this, too?" Rachel asked.

"Perhaps. It's good background information, but it lacks the human touch, the drama of desperate people caught up in a desperate moment."

"What are you going to do now?" Lynn asked.

Good question, thought Samuels. What was he going to do? Where would the quest take him next? Before he could respond, Matt charged in, saying, "What's this, Dad?" He was holding some of my notes, which had fallen to the floor. "It looks like a poem."

"It is. It's called *Phooey on Bluie*. I came across it during my research."

"Who wrote it?" Jan asked.

"Anonymous."

"Read it to us," Rachel piped in. "It sounds like fun."

What could Samuels do? After all the serious stuff, perhaps a little humor wouldn't hurt. He gathered himself and read a whimsical piece of history.

You've read of the brave Russian Stalingrad stand,
How the Axis were chased through the North African sand,
But speaking of battlers, we know there are none
To compare with our winter at Bluie West One.

The mountains of Greenland rise into the sky
As a field of the fjord where the ice drifts by.
The worst of it is, with its infinite trails,
There isn't a woman within one thousand miles.

Halfway to London in later 'forty-two,
Wait eighteen Marauders for skies to turn blue.
It's said that they serve who just sit and wait,
And yet a war's lost with too little, too late.

Then get out the cards, boys, and shake up the dice;
You're better off here than up on the ice!
When you're down on the cap, they say, "Just sit tight,"
Yet some guys sit still for the fortieth night.

Perhaps we're too critical; there are good features, too!
But rule out the mess with its eternal stew,
And cross off the permanent officers here,
The brief fleeting daylight, the shortage of beer.
Only hermits and llamas can do without sex,
So give us good weather and we're fly on to "X."
To us, just one place in the world really rates,
So let's finish the war and get back to the States!

"I like it," Rachel exclaimed."

"What's that part about sex and hermits, Dad?" Matt questioned.

"Your father will explain things later," Lynn chimed in. "Later."

"Glad you liked it, guys."

"Dad, you never said what you're going to do next?" Rachel said.

"I'm going to try to find a cook named Big Hit."

"Do I get to hear about the hermits and sex, too?" Kieran asked, curiosity written all over his inquiring face. "Sounds interesting."

CHAPTER 12

MEETINGS

MID-MARCH – 1962 – WASHINGTON D.C.

The Director was angry. Brady and Hill could see that. Dressed in one of his many somber gray suits, and with his hair combed straight back, J. Edgar Hoover looked like a foaming Irish Bull Dog as he stormed around his grand office. His voice was raw from yelling at his underlings. Beads of sweat dotted his forehead. For a man usually under control, he was punching the air to make a point, or stabbing his agents with colorful words, and elaborate descriptions of the exotic places they would be transferred to if things didn't improve.

"What the hell is going on?" Hoover shouted.

"You know what we know," Brady replied. "You've read the transcript of Samuels' meeting with Epstein."

"The 'bug' worked perfectly," Hill added.

Unsatisfied with their comments, Hoover charged into them, almost accusing the two agents of incompetency, or worst of all, insufficient loyalty to the Bureau, that is, to the Director.

"I'm not sure I can count of you, Hill," Hoover barked at the agent. "Can I count of you, my Jewish agent, to deal with Samuels?"

"I'm a professional, sir. You know that," Hill countered.

"One, I might add, who has not always shown unmitigated support for the Bureau's policy," Hoover snarled.

"I do my job," Hill said, trying to reassure his boss.

"We'll see."

The Director, as if on cue, sat down at his oversized desk. He pulled out a pink handkerchief, which he used to wipe his brow and lips. He poured himself a glass of water and slowly drank half the glass. He didn't offer any to the two agents now standing before him. Based on previous experience, they hadn't expected any amenities. Hoover adjusted his thin black tie before placing his paw-like hands on the desk, palms down.

"Tell me again about this 'Big Hit." person."

"It's all in our report," Brady said pleasantly. "This guy was a cook on the *Dorchester* for at least three years before the military took over the ship from the cruise line."

"His real name is Morris Jones," Hill added. "He was a prize fighter before becoming a cook. Apparently, he was pretty good."

"Yes, I know all that," Hoover said. "Anything else?"

"He seems to have been close to the *Dorchester's* captain, "Brady explained.

"I aware of that. I did read your report."

"Jones' closest friend was another cook by the name of Cookie," Hill volunteered.

"Yes, yes. Nothing else?"

"Morris' body was never found, Hill pointed out. "The last anyone saw of him," Brady said, "he was standing next to the Captain on the main deck handing out life jackets."

"Near the Chaplains? "Hoover asked sharply.

"It appears so," Hill said.

"That's all you have?"

"Just one other thing," Brady murmured.

"And that is?"

"Jones was a Negro."

The word hung in the air. "Jones was a Negro." The Director hadn't known that.

"That wasn't in your report," he said flatly to the agents. "Why was that?"

"An oversight," Hill said quietly.

"Our mistake," Brady said warily. "We didn't think it was important."

"Obviously," the Director snapped.

Hoover mulled over what he had heard. Though no longer a field agent, his instincts roamed far beyond bureaucratic management of the FBI. He was thinking through what he had heard.

The Kennedys got Kurtz to investigate the sinking of the *Dorchester*. Why? Kurtz convinces a reporter, Robert Samuels, to investigate the matter and to write a book. Why? The reporter visits a photographer and a *Dorchester* survivor? Why? According to the latest reports, Samuels is planning to visit Jones' family in Mississippi. Why would he do that? He's also planning to see relatives of the *Dorchester's* Captain in San Diego. Again, why?

What was Samuels looking for? What was he trying to prove? No, what was he trying to confirm? What was Kurtz up to? Why were the Kennedys so interested in the *Dorchester*?

The Director rethought his questions. He was missing something. He turned the questions around. If Jones, a Negro, died very much like the Chaplains, passing out life jackets, why would that be important to the Kennedys? It might make the late news, but then what? The Kennedys were already doing well with the Negro vote. The Administration was already pursuing a civil rights bill, which it hoped to pass through Congress in the coming year. Could there be a connection?

Hoover let the question hang for a moment. Chaplains, he thought, plus a Negro cook, equal what? More sentiment for Negro, was that what this was all about? Possibly. Sentiment to help pass the emerging civil rights legislation? That was very possible. Hell, that's what the Kennedys are up to, using a black man's past to pass their white man's policy to change the social structure of the country. Instead of fighting the communists and domestic threats, they're pushing their liberal agenda. Damn New Englanders, why can't they leave well enough alone?

"So that's it," Hoover said aloud.

"What?" Hill asked.

Hoover glanced at his agents. Could they be trusted to carry out his wishes? So close to retirement, they would have no other choice.

"This is what I want you to do. First, continue to follow Samuels. Second, if necessary, deter him from his investigation. Third, intimidate him. If that doesn't work, stop him from completing his research."

"Deter him?" Hill asked.

"Precisely."

"Intimidation?" Brady questioned.

"Within the law, of course. And another thing, the KKK is following Samuels. Protect his backside for now. Any questions?"

The two agents had many questions. However, they knew better than to bring them up. Retirement was indeed on the horizon. Still...

While Hoover was meeting with his agents, the Source found himself, along with Kurtz and the President's press secretary, conferring with Robert Kennedy in the old Justice Building. The Attorney-General was a bundle of hot Irish nerves. His shirt collar was open and his sleeves were rolled up. His red and black Harvard tie was loose. Waving his arms and speaking in a staccato voice, Kennedy moved around the room at frantic pace. With his tousled hair, he looked and acted like a political whirlwind in motion.

"Okay, I've the reports," Kennedy snapped. "You've done a good job, Kurtz. But what does it all mean? I can't tell if Samuels is making any real progress concerning a Fifth Chaplain."

"Sir, I think he is," Kurtz responded. "Though circumstantial, it appears that he has a lead, which he'll follow up in Mississippi and San Diego."

"You mean, this guy 'Big Hit?'"

"Yes, Morris Jones," Kurtz said. "There's good reason to think he was handling out life jackets in the proximity of the Chaplains."

"What's in Mississippi?" the Attorney-General asked.

"Morris has a sister there," Kurtz reminded him.

"And San Diego?"

"A relative of the Captain lives there."

"That's?"

"Hans J. Danielsen," the skipper of the *Dorchester*."

"The Captain's body was never found, right?"

"Correct."

The Attorney-General finally sat down, scribbled a few notes, and then turned to the Source. "Mr. Fairfield, what kind of backup were we giving Samuels?"

The Source was almost caught off guard. It was seldom that anyone asked him anything. At times, it seemed that no one even remembered he was around. It was strange to hear his name called. Usually, he sat quietly in the background providing necessary documents or confidential information for Kurtz. Like wallpaper, he liked being present, but not really seen. He was most happy being a nondescript bureaucrat. Today, however, was different. His name had been called.

"The FBI has two agents shadowing him. They've sending complete reports to me, which I've shared with Mr. Kurtz. These reports are also going to the Bureau. As per your request, Hoover seems to be playing ball."

"Does he suspect what the President is up to?"

"Difficult to know," the Source suggested, but very little gets past him."

"Would he jam the works if he knew?" Kennedy asked.

The Source didn't want to answer that question. But with everyone looking at him, he had no choice.

"The Director, perhaps because of his Southern upbringing, is sympathetic to those who want to maintain the present social order."

"Separate but unequal," Kennedy said.

"Yes. He also equates the civil rights movement with the international communist movement. He considers King, for example, to be a potential domestic threat. He's concerned about King encouraging and supporting demonstrations and boycotts."

"Any other happy news?"

"Hoover wants to keep the Bureau pure?"

"What the hell does that mean?"

"To the extent he can, he limits the number of Negroes, Jews, and women in the FBI. He also bypasses these groups when it comes to promotions."

"Christ, he thinks he's running his own fiefdom," Kennedy said sourly.

"He is doing just that," the Source said.

Kennedy ran his hands through he hair and rubbed his eyes before speaking in a low voice. "Fairfield, I expect you to monitor the Bureau."

"As you wish, Sir."

Kennedy now turned to Kurtz. "These reports from the FBI agents are very concise, very complete, almost as if they were listening on Samuels' interviews."

"Yes, very complete, Sir."

"Is the Bureau bugging these interviews?"

"It's possible."

"Christ Almighty!"

The Attorney-General got up and walked over to the Source.

"Mr. Fairfield, you're from the South."

"Tennessee, to be exact. A border state, Sir."

"Of course. You are aware, I'm sure of Southern sensitivities concerning the recent civil rights demonstrations."

"Certainly."

"Well, here's my question. Do you think the KKK would hinder, perhaps even harm Samuels if they knew what he was doing?"

The irony of the question was not lost on the Source. How to respond was, however, his main concern.

"The KKK's ideology does not accept the mixing of the races. It's hard to predict how far the Klan would go to maintain the status quo."

"I agree with you. So gentlemen, let's take very good care of our Mr. Samuels. I don't want anything to happen to him."

Two hours after their meeting with the Director, Hall and Brady were having lunch at the Golden Dragon, reputed to have the best Chinese food outside of Georgetown.

The owner was Robert E. Lee, a third generation son of an immigrant who came to America in the 1870's to work for the Union Pacific Railroad as a black powder "blaster." The youthful first Lee saved his money and settled in San Francisco, where he ran a laundry and eventually a small hotel catering to Asians. It was there that he married his "picture bride," who arrived by steamship from Shanghai.

The second Lee continued the family business before traveling to Washington D.C. to get away from San Francisco and other California cities, which had passed Asian restrictive acts to prohibit Chinese and Japanese children from attending public schools. Real or not, the threat of the "yellow peril" had been let loose in the state. In the nation's capitol, however, he worked hard and eventually opened up the Golden Dragon and prospered. There he married a charming girl from Hong Kong. When their son Robert was born, he was named Robert E. Lee. The "E" stood for Edgar, because his mother loved the Tarzan books and movies.

Taking advantage of his name, the third Lee claimed to have the best "sweet and sour pork ribs" in the South. For Lee, the South was anything outside of the Mall area. His loyal customers seemed to agree with his rib claims, and were sympathetic when it came to his sense of direction.

Brady and Hall were seated in a private booth in back of the restaurant. A flimsy drawn curtain gave them the illusion of seclusion, even as the sweet aromas of the kitchen drifted by, onions, chicken frying, and spicy vegetables cooking in hot oil. Their table was a collection of ribs, rice, scrimp, and Blue Moon, an excellent Shanghai beer.

"Damn good food," Brady remarked. "Damn good."

"Old Robert E. Lee knows the secret," Hill said with delight.

"Have another beer, old buddy," Brady said warmly. "You can use it to wash away our conversation with the Director."

"He always brings up the Jewish thing," Hill muttered.

"That's because he likes you."

"Brady, you're full of B.S."

"True enough. The bastard always brings up the retirement issue, or where he'll send us in Alaska if we screw off."

"Speaking of screwing off, what are we going to do about Samuels? "Hill asked flatly.

Brady was about to answer when the curtain was drawn back and the proprietor, Robert E. Lee, smiling face and all, stood their holding a dessert tray.

"Gentlemen, our finest green tea ice cream and fortune cookies guaranteeing success in all your endeavors."

"Guaranteed success, you say," Brady mused. "We could use some of that."

"Then enjoy, my friends."

The curtain closed before Hill spoke again. "What about Samuels?"

"Balance... We to find a balance point."

"Explain, please."

"We'll cover the guy's back," Brady said, "especially if the KKK is involved," he continued. "We'll hinder his investigation if we're convinced national security is in play."

"No rough stuff," Hill protested.

"Hopefully, not. Now enjoy your ice cream, while I check my fortune."

Brady cracked open his cookie, read the enclosed message, then began to laugh, deeply and heartily.

"What's up?" Hill asked.

"The cookie must know something. It's telling me to prepare for an exciting adventure."

The Source exited his office at noon and found a nearby pay phone. He quickly dialed his number. A moment later, Stretch came on the line.

"It's me," the Source said.

"What news?" Stretched asked.

Kurtz and the Attorney-General know there's a KKK tail."

At his end of the line, Stretch nodded. "We figured they catch on to us. Any change of plans?"

"Follow and observe, and no rough stuff, at least for now. Make sure Baldy and Nails understand. Samuels is headed for San Diego and then Mississippi. And watch out for the FBI."

"No rough stuff... Baldy will be truly disappointed."

CHAPTER 13

THE CAPTAIN

LATE MARCH 1962 – SAN DIEGO

Robert Samuels had made the decision, actually three decisions. After considerable pressure from his lovely wife, what might be called nudging by any other name, he caved in and decided to take her with him to San Diego to meet a relative of Captain Hans J. Danielsen, who was the skipper of the *Dorchester*. That would mean leaving the kids alone at home, always a questionable thing to do. But their promises to "be good" won the day, plus their mother was siding with them. Of course, she get Kieran to promise to keep his cousins out of trouble. Four to one were poor odds to fight. Samuels cashed in his cards. The nice part was their decision to drive rather than fly. In this way, the trip would be a bit of a vacation from the stress of searching for the "Fifth Chaplain."

The drive down the coast to Los Angeles was great. They spent the first night in Monterey, where they enjoyed a wonderful fish dinner, wild salmon, a baked potato overflowing with butter and chives, and French beans seasoned just right. Hot apple pie proved the final satisfying touch. The Monterey Seaside Inn provided a romantic view of the Pacific, which, as the fleeing guardians of three teen-agers, they embraced heartily.

Continuing along Highway I, they drove to Big Sur and the beautiful strand of Redwoods, which made the area so attractive

93

to tourists. Moving on, they drove for over 100 miles to the Hearst Castle, a testament to what "yellow journalism" can buy when one wants a lasting monument to his achievements. And William Randolph Hearst certainly desired that. The newspaper publisher spared few pennies in collecting the world's art to furnish his own personal museum. Samuels wondered if he could have worked for such a guy? He left the question open. They spent the night in Cambria, a few miles south of the "castle." The next day it was on to Santa Barbara, the beautiful mission there and another fish dinner off State Street. The following day would take them to the "city of Angels," a visit to Hollywood, and a charming hotel in Santa Monica.

As Samuels drove, he reflected on his good luck. He had an absolutely fantastic wife, smart, supportive, beautiful, a good cook, and a thoroughly modern mom. Rachel, their oldest child, was a long-haired beauty, who had a mind of her own, and an intellect allowing her to do well in school. Matthew, tall and lean, and athletic as hell, enjoyed football and basketball, though baseball was his first love. Somehow, he found a way to play ball and pass his classes. And now with Kieran, he had, at least temporarily, a whiz on the computer and a thoughtful kid, He was a joy to be around. Yes, Samuels was lucky and he knew it.

Leaving Santa Monica, Samuels drove southward on Interstate 405, which eventually joined the 5, and the most direct route to San Diego and Mission Bay, where William Neilson had consented to meet with him. Indeed, the man seemed overjoyed to finally know someone was interested in his distant relative.

Mission Bay is perhaps San Diego's most popular outdoor destination. It is really a complex of waterfront parks, spacious public beaches, and recreational paths for bike riders and walkers stretching some 27 miles of golden, sunny shoreline. It was a place for picnics, bird watching, and water sports, especially jet skis, motorboats, and toy-like sailboats tacking to the wind. William Neilson had chosen a great place to live.

It turned out that Neilson lived in the Sunset Cove Trailer Park in a large pre-fabricated home just a few feet from the bay. He greeted Samuels and his wife warmly.

"You made good time. Welcome to Sunset Cove."

Neilson was a big man, well over six feet, middle aged, and powerfully built. One could see in his long blond hair and sparkling blue eyes not only a Dane, but a Viking in the mold of Erik the Red. His extended hand was large, calloused, and by appearances, strong. Fortunately, he took mercy on Samuels' rather puny offering. As for Lynn, he bowed deeply and, taking her hand, he kissed her on both cheeks. Neilson, it seemed, was not only a Viking, but a romantic Norseman to boot.

"You must be Mrs. Samuels. It's a pleasure to meet you."

"As I am to meet with you."

Inside the house, Neilson guided Samuels and his wife into the living room, which, while well decorated with fine furniture and exquisite area carpets, seemed more like a library, bookcases, overflowing with of all things books, journals, and magazines clung to each wall. A cursory glance indicated Neilson was a dedicated World War II buff with a special interest in naval history.

What caught Samuels' eye was a ship model on the coffee table.

"You like it?" Neilson asked.

"Very much.

"It took me almost two years to make it."

"Why so long?" Jas asked.

"I had to find copies of the original blueprints of the *Dorchester*," Neilson said, "and then I to determine a ratio I could work with in constructing the model."

"The details are amazing."

"Accuracy and precision demanded concentration and patience."

"You did your work well," Samuels said with joy in his voice. "Just look at this. It looks like it could just float away if given half a chance."

The model was about 40 inches long, perhaps six inches wide, and highly detailed in all aspects as Samuels had noted. The 20mm guns were placed exactly where they had been on the *Dorchester*. The lifeboats and doughnut rafts were positioned correctly. The long graceful lines of the ship told of a cruise liner carrying well-heeled passengers up the Atlantic Coast, and later, voyaging across the Atlantic bearing young men to an uncertain destiny. One could almost hear seaman yelling, "Cast off those lines."

Samuels found himself drawn to the model. He peered at it intensely, as if somehow he was trying to board the old ship. He felt himself wanting to walk her top deck and grab onto the teak railings. He wanted to feel the ship vibrate under his feet as the great engines fired up and propelled the ship forward. He could feel, he thought, the ship cutting through the water, leaving a foaming white wake behind her.

He couldn't help himself.

Samuels gently touched the model, running his hand down the keel, while his fingers caressed the lifeboats. He peered directly at the bridge, as if trying to stand by the captain, perhaps even to grip the wheel in the steering house. He wanted to take in the view of the bow plowing ahead into the darkened waves, always moving forward at the urging of the great engines deep within the ship. He wanted to see and feel the spray of salty ocean water splashing up against the bridge window, and along side of the ship, foaming water pushed aside by metal from Pittsburg. He wanted to taste black coffee, hot and steaming, delivered in a thick, white mug. He wanted to know his feet trod on the *Dorchester's* planks.

Inwardly and quite unexpectedly, Samuels shuddered. He realized he was looking at more than a fine replica of a ship. This was the *USAT Dorchester* itself, a living, breathing creature of steel and steam. He could hear the usual griping of soldiers far from home. He could see Captain pacing the wheelhouse, imploring his ship to hold steady in the convoy. He could hear the comforting words of the Chaplains exorcising the demons of fear and fright of the men as the ship sailed into dangerous waters. He felt the torpedo explosion rumbling through the ship. He could see the sailors desperately chipping away at ice-covered ropes and pulleys from which hung the lifeboats. He felt the dread of men jumping overboard into a frozen sea. And then he tasted the salt water, which took away his breath, a cold hand gripping his chest, threatening to end all that he knew of this world. It was then that he knew the fear of impending death as he had never known it.

"Dear, are you okay?" Lynn asked.

Samuels felt a dark cloud passing over him as he continued to touch the ship. Sweat broke out on his forehead. His fingers trembled, even as his heart pounded against his chest. He found himself wanting to grip the ship tightly and then he heard his own voice yelling, "No!"

Rushing over to his guest, Neilson said, "Mr. Samuels, let me help you. Please let go of the model and sit down."

Neilson's words fell on deaf ears. Samuels remained anchored to the ship. Nelson repeated the request, now more an order. Still Samuels clung to the model ship. Using his powerful, strong hands, Neilson finally broke Samuels' grip on the model and helped him to the couch.

"Robert, what happened?" Lynn asked.

"You won't believe it. I felt the torpedo hitting the ship." Samuels said. "I heard the screams as water rushed into the engine room. I saw the men wounded and dying. I saw them jumping into the water so cold that not even snow flakes melt in it. I felt the terror gripping the men. I could feel the ship beginning its last slow slide into the sea."

"A drink is what you need," Neilson declared.

"For all of us," Lynn said. "Robert, you need a drink."

"I saw them. The Chaplains. On the top deck... Handing out life preservers and their gloves. Just giving them away... Trying desperately to keep the men calm. Four of them... And then another... A big man..."

Neilson quickly hurried to the kitchen. He returned with glasses for three and two bottles of wine.

"Mrs. Samuels?"

"White, please."

"Mr. Samuels?"

Samuels' voice answered, but not in a way Neilson expected. As he did so, tears ran down his face.

"I saw them. I heard them, the Chaplains. "They were praying with the men,"

"Robert…"

"I saw them holding hands. I heard them singing. I could feel their faith."

Samuels was crying now, long soft sobs of pain and understanding. He looked at his wife, hoping she could comprehend what he had just experienced, expecting her to understand.

"I saw the Captain and the cook. They had handed out the last of the life jackets, including their own. They were resigned to their fate. They had a look of acceptance. For a moment, they caught the attention of the Chaplains. Together, seemed to acknowledge some personal and special truth. And then they were gone."

Across the street from Neilson's house, a truck was parked. The lettering on it said Ace's Plumbing. Inside the truck, no tools of the trade could be found. Instead, costly state-of-the-art listening and recording equipment occupied space. Two FBI agents were listening intently as Samuels, unknowingly was being bugged and recorded.

"Jesus, did you hear all that Hill?" Brady asked.

"How could I miss it, perfect bug, perfect sound?"

"What the hell is going on?"

"Something beyond us," Hill said with disbelief in his words.

"Wait until Hoover hears this," Brady said.

Samuels was calmer now. Two glasses of red wine and cheese crackers with tasty slices of spicy salami, plus the reassuring voice of Lynn seemed to do that. It also helped that Neilson was now talking about his relative.

"You can see from my library that the Second World War has captured my imagination and a good deal of my money. I've read at least 3,000 books, many of them dealing with the merchant marine and troop ships. Sadly, very little is written about the *Dorchester*, and even less about Han J. Danielsen."

"What can you tell us?" Lynn asked.

"Here's the only picture I have of him."

Neilson handed Lynn an old black and white photograph. It showed a strong face wearing an officer's hat and looking sternly at the camera. He was wearing a full winter uniform and a wool jacket.

"I've been told," Neilson said, "that he had sky-blue eyes and iron-gray hair, which he brushed straight back in a kind of chopped style."

"He looks like a Viking," Lynn said.

"His parents came from Denmark. He was born in the USA."

"How old is he in the picture?" Samuels asked.

"Early 50's from what I can tell. He had already been at sea for over 22-years, and he had made the run from St. John's to Greenland many times. But was his first time as master of the *Dorchester*."

"First and last time," Lynn said remorsefully.

"Regrettably, yes. I liked to think he loved the old ship. You know, the *Dorchester* wasn't built for high seas. It wasn't a blue water ship. She cruised the Gulf of Mexico and the eastern seaboard, mainly coastal runs. With its costly teak railings and trim silhouette, she was meant to be a pricy steamer for the affluent who wanted a short holiday. With the coming of the war, she was drafted into the military as a troop ship, thus its designation, a United Sates Army Troopship. She was built to carry 325 passengers.

The night she was sunk, 900 men were crowded aboard her. Four of the passengers had bunked in cabin B-14."

"The Four Chaplains?" Lynn asked.

"Yes. How did you know?"

"Female intuition."

"Of course. They were so close, only 150 miles from Greenland, just one night, and one full day of steaming and they would have made it to safety. Radar on the command ship picked up German subs trailing the convoy. Planes were requested to patrol over the convoy, but none was available, certainly, none that could fly at night. The best Captain Danielsen could do was warn his passengers of the danger, which he did when they entered torpedo junction, where the subs lurked. He asked everyone to sleep in their in their uncomfortable and warm life jackets. He doubled the lookouts. The Navy gunners attached to the ship were at their stations. All that could be done was done. He even agreed to invoke prayer."

"Prayer!" Samuels said in a startled manner.

"One of the survivors, a radar officer, overheard the Chaplains and the Captain praying. They were holding hands in a circle."

"Beseeching god?" Lynn asked.

"Seeking help beyond what radar and guns could provide," Samuels added, emotion coloring his words.

"It was almost as if they knew this was their last night on earth," Neilson said in a somber voice. "Almost as if they knew."

Neilson opened up a thick folder and pulled out a crumpled piece of paper with thick, heavy writing on it. In places, the ink had been smeared in the past.

"Here it is," he announced. "This prayer, as remembered by the officer, was given by Rabbi Goode on behalf of all the Chaplains."

God of our fathers and of all the earth, you are both master of the seas and master of our hearts. I ask your special blessing on Captain Danielsen, the Dorchester, and everyone o n board. Keep us from fear of anything except our power. Give us the resolve and the courage to meet whatever challenge lies ahead. Give us the calm that comes from knowing everything we do is for your glory. Give Captain Danielsen the assurance every day that he is guided and protected by your all-powerful hand. We lift him up to you. Amen.

Dabbing her eyes, Lynn said, "I never heard a more beautiful prayer."

Samuels could only nod in agreement. The words transcended all, yet connected everyone to a living God, which in this moment, not even a faint-hearted agnostic could deny. If words could be music, this was a symphony of hope for a better world if one could but find the courage to make it.

"Mr. Samuels, a question."

"Yes?"

"I've read your first two articles about the *Dorchester*, which were printed in the *San Francisco Chronicle*. Are you going to follow them up with a story about the Captain?"

"Yes. Oh, yes. With great joy, I intend write about good man and a special prayer."

"I'll look forward to it."

"Robert, haven't we forgotten something. Big Hit, we're hear to learn about him, aren't we, Lynn asked.

"Big Hit?" Neilson inquired.

"There was a cook aboard the *Dorchester*," Samuels said. "Some called him "Big Hit." His real name was Morris Jones, a very large man, a Negro. I believe he was a close friend of Captain Donielsen. Ever come across his name?"

"Possible. According to the radar officer, I mentioned earlier, he saw the Captain, who had been hurt when the torpedo exploded, being helped by a Negro on the main deck. This man Morris, I think. Apparently, the Captain was handing out life jackets, while issuing commands, and was unsteady on his feet. What do you think?"

"Could be," Samuels said. "But I need more information. I need confirmation. I need to speak to this radar officer."

"He lives in Pensacola, Florida, on the 'panhandle.' I'll find you his number."

Samuels looked again at the model ship. For a moment, he was again lost in the waves of history. To no one in particular, he said, "Will I have the resolve and the courage to meet the challenges ahead to find, if he exists, the "Fifth Chaplain."

"What did you say?" Lynn asked.

"I guess I'm going to Mississippi to find out about a lost cook and then to Florida to find a sonar guy."

CHAPTER 14

THE DEEP SOUTH

APRIL 1962 – PASCAGOULA, MISSISSIPPI

Robert Samuels, after returning home from San Diego, took two weeks off at the insistence of his wife. It was more an edict than a recommendation.

"You're going to rest and relax, Robert, so don't even think about traveling to Mississippi until I give you the green light."

"Mississippi and Florida, Lynn."

"I don't care if it's the entire "Old Confederacy.""

"I'll fall behind on my schedule."

"Good! That's better than you falling down."

"You're a tyrant!"

"And you better do what I say if you know what's good for you."

Inwardly, Samuels knew his wife was right. He was exhausted, not only from the travel, but from the interviews. Uncomfortable issues were being raised about the *Dorchester's* sinking. Had the Navy provided enough escort ships to better protect the convoy on the jog from St. John's to Greenland? Were there sufficient life jackets and boats for the overloaded ship? Why did chasing after a German sub take precedent over saving men from a frozen hell? Was there really a "Fifth Chaplain?" If so, would his existence actually help the President with his impending civil rights legislation?

His experience with the replica of the *Dorchester* had a profound effect on him. He couldn't quite put into words, though he was trying as he wrote his next article for the *Chronicle*. Something beyond words had occurred. His empathetic sensitivities had been aroused. He had felt --- more than seen --- the Captain, the Chaplains, and Big-Hit. On some level, he bonded with them, which helped him to understand the mixture of realism and faith, which kept them from faltering as they ministered to others and accepted their fate. The Captain would not leave his stricken ship and Big-Hit would not leave the Captain. The Chaplains would not, could not, forsake the privilege to serve a loving God even as the *Dorchester* slipped beneath the waves.

Robert Samuels understood all this now. But how to write about his experience was the great challenge. Would his readers think he had gone off the deep end?

Psychologists might call all this a "peak experience," some transcending moment when the bounds of earthly restraints are thrown to the wind. Theologians might suggest he had a mystical experience, a spiritual moment of oneness, where dualities faded in the absence of a subject-object relationship.

Samuels felt emotionally drained. He needed time to recoup. Yes, his wife was right. Difficult as it might be, he would use the two weeks to write a third story for the *Chronicle*, this time about Captain Hans T. Donielsen and the replica of the *Dorchester* in San Diego. He would not shy away from what happened in San Diego. His editor proved to be enthusiastic. The stories about the *Dorchester* had caught on with the public.

"Keep them coming, Samuels," the editor said. "People are really into this story,"

"You're sure?"

"Just check the letters to the editors. People want to know more about the Chaplains? What kind of men were they? Why did the sacrifice their lives? You've touched a nerve."

Secretly, Samuels was immensely delighted the stories were doing so well. More stories would follow, that he knew, but only after some "R & R." He needed the time to enjoy his children, to watch his son pitch against Lincoln High School, to enjoy political chitchat with his daughter as they washed and dried the dishes. And he wanted more time with Kieran, his unplanned for but wonderful visitor, even if only on a temporary basis. He needed the time to once more enjoy the safety and security of his home, and the wife who made it so. In short, he needed all that the Chaplains had so unselfishly given up as they made the ultimate sacrifice.

As so often happens, an unexpected remark led to one of the kids surprising him, almost knocking him out of this chair at dinner. He had always encouraged his kids to use the dinnertime to discuss what was on their minds, whether politics, their next vacation, or what was happening in school. Even what their father was writing about. And why? It was a way of keeping the family grounded. On the same page, communicating with each other. It began with Rachel asking, "We really don't know much about the *Dorchester*, do we? I mean about the ship itself. What was it like before the tragedy?"

"With zest to his comment, Matt added, "Yeah. What was the ship like, Dad? You're the expert."

"I'm afraid I'm just learning about the ship. Can't add much."

To everyone's surprise, Lynn said, I know someone who can help us."

"Who?" Samuels asked.

"Kieran."

Everyone stared at the husky kid with blazing blue eyes, and brown hair many would die for.

"Ask him, Robert."

"Kieran, what's up?"

"I've been doing some research on my own, Kieran answered somewhat sheepishly. Mrs. Samuels helped me."

"Aunt Lynn, Kieran."

"And? Samuels questioned.

"I need to get my notebook, Mr. Samuels."

"Uncle Bob, Kieran."

With that, Kieran dashed to his room, returning a moment later with his new notebook. He opened it, checked the faces at the table, and began to talk, haltingly at first, then with greater confidence. It helped that Aunt Lynn supported him with an encouraging smile.

"First, the *Dorchester* was built for the Merchants and Miners Transportation Company in 1926. The Newport News Shipbuilding and Dry Dock Company actually built the ship, which was launched on March 20, 1926. The ship was really a passenger liner carrying up to 314 passengers in luxury on cruises to cities such as Baltimore, Philadelphia, and Boston besides Miami, Jacksonville, and Savannah."

"Luxury?" Matt asked more than said.

"Each room had electric fans and telephones. There was an onboard freezer for making ice cream. The ship had a dance pavilion on the boat deck and music was provided from in the morning and evening. There were live recitals conducted in a special music room. Even radio broadcasts were played when conditions permitted."

"Sounds good to me," Rachel declared.

"The ship also provided deck games and card games. As to gambling in such activities, I couldn't find any information."

"Bet they did," Matt said strongly. "People with lots of money gamble."

"Maybe that's why Dad doesn't," Lynn said with a shy smile, causing her children to laugh heartily.

"Thanks," Samuels uttered under his breath. It's nice to be appreciated."

"No pouting, Robert," Lynn responded. "Go on, Kieran."

"Passengers were able to send wireless messages, something new for that time. Three meals were provided each day, as well as a 'night lunch' between 9:00 and 11:00 each evening. Besides all this, the ship had a barber shop and passengers could even store their automobiles in the cargo hold."

"Well done, Kieran," Samuels proclaimed. "You've really done some researching."

"There's more, Robert" Lynn added, "Tell us, Kieran."

"As were most U.S. passenger ships, the *Dorchester* was converted into a troop carrier after Pearl Harbor. She was outfitted with additional lifeboats and life rafts. The windows in the pilothouse on the bridge were reduced in size to protect the sailors and officers. The ship was also armed with four 20mm guns, one 3-inch 50-caliber gun, and one 4-inch 50-caliber. All of this was done in New York City by the Atlantic, Gulf and West Indies Company. The new troop carrier was launched on January 24, 1942. She was now capable of carrying 906 people, crew and passengers.

"I'm astounded," Samuels remarked. "You did all that on your own." Wow. Maybe you should consider being a newspaper reporter."

"Aunt Lynn pushed me. Made me go to the college library with her. Look at old, dusty books. And read... And read..."

"She can be persistent."

"I'm glad she did."

"Cool," Rachel and Matt said, almost in unison.

"Kieran, the last three things we learned; I think everyone should know, don't you?"

"The German torpedo killed the *Dorchester's* generating power. Because of this, she couldn't send a distress signal. The loss of 667 men was the third worse loss of life at leas for the country during the war. On January 18, 1961, the Congress authorized President Dwight D. Eisenhower to aware the *Dorchester's* chaplains with a new medal, a Special Medal for Heroism. Initially, the Congress wanted to award the chaplains the Medal of Honor. That wasn't possible because that medal is specifically designated for acts of heroism committed under fire in combat."

"Being torpedoed doesn't count," Matt asked with furor coating his words. "That certainly was combat."

"I agree," Rachel piped in. "Giving up your life jackets and gloves... Government bureaucracy... Ugh..."

Later in the evening Samuels received a phone call from Kurtz. He had been expecting it.

"Anything you have on "Big Hit," and the radar officer, I need sooner than later."

"Morris Jones and Aubrey Burch? Kurtz" asked.

"Yes."

"Give me a few days."

"Fine. I can use the time out."

"By the way, the President is enjoying your articles."

"Kennedy reads the *Chronicle?*"

"Only when you're writing."

"How nice."

"At first the Kennedys were unsure about the exposure."

"Why?"

"They had hoped to keep some of this under the radar."

"But?"

"The public interest has floored them. Keep writing."

"As you say..."

A few days later, a thick folder was delivered to Samuels' home by a nondescript public servant, who merely said, "For you, sir," after checking Samuels identification. "Mr. Kurtz sends his compliments."

Samuels went over the enclosed papers and documents with his wife, who was now in this quest up to her apron.

"Okay, it's time for you to go. "I'll pack your things and call the airlines. You make the appointments, my dear reporter."

And that's how Samuels found himself on a Delta jet-prop plane few days later traveling to Memphis, Tennessee.

Though it was only April, Memphis was experiencing, as was the whole region, unusually humid weather, hot, sticky, and draining on one's energy. Samuels found himself damp and sweating all the time. Cold drinks and a paper fan provided by a local mortuary did little to relieve his discomfort. The weary window air conditioning units in his motel, try as they might, provided little respite from the heat.

Unfortunately, there was no direct flight from San Francisco to his destination. He would spend one night in Memphis, which he promised to revisit during the next ice age. From there, Samuels hopped on a vintage Tri-State DC-3, which carried him to Jackson, Mississippi. An Avis rental car, a Plymouth two-door coupe with a rag top, was waiting him at the airport for his next jog, this time on land down US 49 to Hattiesburg, once in consideration for the Mississippi's t capitol. As he drove, he saw grand Spanish moss laden live oaks and splendid ante-bellum structures, and numerous plantations, all reminders of the "lost cause." From Hattiesburg, he motored southward on US 98 to US 63, and finally to US 90.

And that brought him to his destination, Pascagoula, a coastal town halfway between Mobile, Alabama and Biloxi, Mississippi. Robert Samuels was in the Deep South.

A good reporter does his research in advance. He doesn't walk into something ignorant and naïve, if possible. Samuels was a very good reporter. He knew that Hernando De Soto had explored the area in the 1540's, and that Pascagoula meant "bread eaters," according the native-Americans. The later white settlers referred to the area as the "singing river." Apparently, the natives had drowned themselves in the river rather than submit to slavery. They were singing as they died. Information is not always enjoyable.

Samuels was learning that all places have names, and names always have a history. In more modern times, the town laid claim to three worthy accomplishments. First, the PTA was founded in Mississippi. Second, shoes were first sold in boxes in pairs at Phil Gilbert's Shoe Parlor on Washington Street in 1884. The third claim was most interesting. President Theodore Roosevelt came to Mississippi in 1901 to go bear hunting. To guarantee the President a good shot, a bear was caught for him, but the Chief Executive refused to fire at the animal, thinking it was either lame or a cub. The news spread rapidly and a toy maker, one Morris Michtom, took advantage of the moment. He made a stuffed bear called the "Teddy Bear," and the rest, as they say, was history.

The town is also Mississippi's premier and busiest port. The state's largest employer, Northrop Grumman, maintains a reputation as "America's shipbuilder." Other industries bolster the local economy, a Chevron refinery, First Chemical Corporation, Mississippi phosphates, and a new oil company, BP/Amoco. In some respects, the town was a thriving brew of oil and chemistry to meet the needs of high-octane gas and plastic in its multitude of uses.

After stopping at a Texaco station for gas, a cold coke, and directions that a thoroughly disbelieving, somewhat suspicious attendant provided, Samuels headed out of town in a generally easterly direction. He passed through the vibrant downtown business section, and past numerous industrial plants before reaching an affluent neighborhood where colonial style homes and lush green lawns dotted the landscape. He continued driving to what the good people called the "colored area."

In no time at all, he found himself, an olive-skin Jew, driving a late model rental car down dusty roads and into a different world, where "separate but equal," was decidedly "unequal, but very separate."

Samuels was in the world the Kennedys hoped to change. He was in the "land of Jim Crow."

Samuels found the small house belonging to Shirley Jones, Morris Jones' sister. The house rose on stilts since it sat in a flood plane. A lovely porch encircled the front, where old, but venerable wood slat rocking chairs resided. A small table was also on the porch, and on it perched a large glass container of cool ice tea. An older woman in her fifties (or possibly older) rocked back and forth on the porch. She waved to him as he parked in the front yard before stepping out into the fine red dust of southern Mississippi.

"You're Mr. Samuels

"I am."

Shirley Jones was a tall woman, almost six feet tall. She was slim, as thin as a toothpick, very much all bone and muscle, a person used to long hours of hard physical work. Her hair, was brushed straight back into a tight bun, and sprinkled through it were patches of gray. She wore a simple cotton dress, splashed with yellow and blue flowers, and a long row of buttons in the front. A pair of worn sandals cradled her feet. From the way she stood up to greet Samuels, it was obvious she was still pretty spry.

"You look like a man who could use a cold drink."

"That I am, Ms. Jones."

"Miss Jones, it is and have a seat."

Samuels sat down and found himself in no time rocking as he drank the ice tea proffered to him.

"This is tough weather for a guy from San Francisco."

"Oh, things haven't even heated up yet. Now in another two months ..."

"How do you folks handle it?"

"Patiently."

"I need fog in my life."

At that, she laughed before turning serious. "I was surprised to get your letter, Mr. Samuels."

"I couldn't reach you by phone."

"No phone. Your letter came to our local general store, and it was forwarded to me."

"I didn't want to come unannounced."

"Very thoughtful of you."

"I am correct, am I not? Samuels asked. You're Morris Jones' older sister?"

"The last member of the family still kicking."

As they talked, children came into the front yard chasing a ball. They waved to Miss. Jones before running off, ball in hand.

"Exactly, why are you here, Mr. Samuels?'

And so Samuels told her about his quest to find the "Fifth Chaplain," and his interviews so far. He told her about the Kennedys' involvement and their desire to see civil rights legislation passed. She listened quietly.

"You think my brother might be the "Fifth Chaplain?"

"Possible. At best, the evidence is circumstantial but I'm continuing to talk to people."

"I don't think so," she said. "My brother knew his *Bible*, and could he preach when given a chance in church. He had a big, bellowing voice, which, when he really wanted to use it, reminded folks of the old-time prophets. *'And the Lord said...'* You get the idea. He could really get the congregation's juices going. He especially loved talking about God with the children. Here was this giant of a man surrounded by little ones on the church floor talking about Noah and the Whale. The kids loved it. He seemed to have a special knack with them. Jesus came alive when he got going. Lots of folks thought he should have gone into the ministry.

"He sounds like a wonderful man," Samuels said.

"He was. Now, how can I help you?"

"Tell me more about Morris."

Miss. Jones closed her eyes and retreated into some space where memories, some bitter, others happy, resided.

"I was the oldest of five kids, just a year ahead of Morris. Our parents were tenant farmers who worked the cotton fields just as their parents had done. As far back as before the Civil War, our family had smelled and walked this land. My mother wanted things to be different for me, and for Morris. She pushed me to do well in school and I was fortunate enough to attend Lincoln University in southern Pennsylvania. The good Methodists, who started the school before Fort Sumter, helped me to become an elementary school teacher. I came home and did that for 30 some years."

Contemplating what he had seen during his drive to Mrs. Morris' house, Samuels knew being a teacher in the segregated South could not have been easy.

"I'm sure you were a good teacher."

"I tried. God knows that. I never married. My students were my family."

"About Morris…"

"My brother was always big and strong, such a powerful man. He was the biggest kid in school, and on the football team. He had a chance to attend Georgia State. The school wanted him to play on its team."

"An all-Negro team?"

"Yes. But Morris wanted to make some money, to help the family. He picked cotton, worked on shrimp boats and laid railroad ties. He even tried wrestling, but it was boxing that caught his eye. He was very good. Some thought he could be another Jack Johnson, or at least have a shot at Joe Lewis. But the gamblers got a hold of him. They wanted him to throw fights, which he wouldn't do. He quit."

"Better to quit than have your legs broken by the mob."

"Morris thought so."

"How did he end up on the *Dorchester*?"

"In a way that was mother's doing. She was an excellent cook. In fact, she worked in the kitchen of some of the wealthiest families, once the cotton was picked. She convinced Morris that he needed a skill, so she taught him how to cook. And he was a natural. It turned out to be his thing, especially cakes and pies. How that man could bake! In time he got a job with different cruise ship lines before Pearl Harbor. He was working on the *Dorchester* when the war broke out."

Samuels' host replenished his ice tea. She then hurried into the house before returning with a large chunk of apple pie.

"I like to think baking runs in our family, Mr. Samuels."

Samuels took a big bite, savoring as he did, the delightful tastes of his spicy apple pie.

"Without a doubt. Baking is a family trait," he said with a big smile.

"You're too kind, dear sir."

"Did Morris ever write to you about the *Dorchester*?"

"Oh, yes. You know, he made that crossing from St. John's to Greenland at least three times before."

"Did he talk about the Captain or the Chaplains?"

"Nothing about the Captain. This was their first trip together. The same for the Chaplains."

Samuels felt downhearted. He had hoped for something tangible, something to support the possibility that Big Hit was the "Fifth Chaplain."

"But Cookie did," Miss Jones said.

"Cookie?"

"Yes, his best friend. He survived the tragedy."

Samuels was dumbfounded. This was a complete surprise to him. He hadn't known about Cookie's survival.

"He made it," Miss Jones said, "but barely. He was almost frozen to death when the Coast Guard plucked him out of the Atlantic. As it was, he lost a leg and three fingers to frost bite."

"You saw him after the war?"

"Of course."

"Where?"

"Why here?"

"Cookie visited you?"

"Lived here until he died. That was back in '55."

"You took care of him?"

"Yes. I had great affection for him, Mr. Abraham Freeman of Knoxville, Tennessee, which was the way he introduced himself to folks."

"He was Morris' best friend?"

"And the only love of my life until he died?"

"I'm so sorry."

"Don't be. The time we had together was special."

"He spoke about the Chaplains?"

"Often. He especially liked the Rabbi."

"Goode?"

"Alexander Goode. Yes. He was the first Jew Cookie ever really knew. And Cookie was the first Negro the Rabbi came to know beyond a superficial level. Together with Morris, they would pray together."

"How extraordinary."

"You know, Cookie had an exceptional memory. He remembered one prayer in particular, which I've never forgotten."

"Perhaps you would read it to me."

"No need, Mr. Samuels."

Miss Jones got up, straightened her back, took a deep breath, and then closed her eyes. For a minute she remained that way before pulling from a deep recess of her mind a prayer, which touched Samuels beyond anything he had heard so far. It would give him the courage to continue the quest.

"We all have the same God, and right now we all have the same enemy. He's out there now, making our lives miserable, or trying to. We can't control whether he breaks our body, only God can do that. But we can control whether he breaks our spirit. And he can't do it if you won't let him. Whatever happens to us on this mission, you can bet your last cent that.

God loves you. Amen.

"That was beautiful."

"Cookie would recite it almost every night."

"Reminding him of the *Dorchester.*"

"Not completely."

"I don't understand."

Miss Jones steadied herself, as if about to give a speech to the nation. And perhaps she was.

"Abraham was fighting two enemies, Mr. Samuels. There was, of course, the Nazi U-boats. Yes, that was the case, brutal and present. What else? You're a reporter, intuitive and curious. What else was on Cookie's mind."

"Jim Crow."

"As I said, you're intuitive. The entire ugly system of prejudice, discrimination, and the "separation of the races based on color... That was the enemy."

"Making your life miserable."

"Reducing our lives to less than equal status. Restrooms for Negroes, drinking fountains for Negroes, rear seats on buses for Negroes. The whole nasty business."

"But they couldn't break you?"

"Exactly, Mr. Samuels. Jim Crow could break our bodies. That's physical. But not our spirit... We won't let the racists do that. We will always fight oppression. Not just against Germany, but here at home, too."

"And God loves you for this effort."

"That is our hope."

Samuels had come to the Deep South to learn about the *Dorchester.* He left Mrs. Jones' home having learned far more than he expected.

CHAPTER 15

THE RADAR OFFICER

APRIL 1962 – GULF BREEZE, FLORIDA

Robert Samuels was feeling pretty good about things as he drove along U.S. 90 toward Gulf Breeze, Florida, not far from Pensacola. Purring along with the ragtop down and the wind brushing through his hair, even the hot, humid air was bearable as he thought about the progress he had made to date.

Circumstantial or not, it appeared more and more that Big Hit, though he was not a clergyman by trade, might still be the "Fifth Chaplain." In some ways, Samuels surmised, that made Jones' story so much more compelling. After all, Chaplains didn't have a monopoly on compassion or faith. And Chaplains, to some degree, were expected to sacrifice in the name of their living God, but a cook, a former prize- fighter, who would expect such person to do so? Yet, without doubt, Big Hit had stood tall and strong against the frightening night skies and fearful dark waters of the Atlantic to calm terrified shipmates. Neglecting his own safety, he had given his lifejacket to another man. All this was increasingly a matter of record.

Samuels had another reason for feeling good today. Taking the strong recommendation of his wife, he had stopped at a Waffle House restaurant in Mobile, Alabama. As she had said on the phone, it would be worth his time.

"Robert, just do it. Take my word for it, the food is fantastic."

"You say, it's easy to find."

"Just look for a sign with a yellow background and bold, black lettering."

"That's it?"

"The restaurant are usually in free-standing buildings, separate from other structures. They resemble 1950's type diners, and they're open 24-hours per day."

"Family style eating?"

"Yes. But never ask for pancakes."

"Why not?"

"They don't serve them. But if you like eggs, grits, and waffles, this is your place."

"What about hash browns, my favorite?"

"Are you in luck, mister... They have the best hash browns in the South."

"No way."

"If I remember correctly, they describe them as 'scattered, smothered, and covered' in their ads."

Samuels did indeed enjoy his breakfast of waffles piled high with butter and topped off with syrup, three scrambled eggs, and golden hash browns beautifully cooked in pecan oil. As he ate, he read a fact sheet offered by his waitress, a college girl of ample proportions and a winning personality. He learned that since 1955, the Waffle House, with over a thousand outlets, had sold:

. over 459,000,000 waffles or 159 waffles per minute.

. more than 950,000,000 cups of coffee or 136 cups per minute.

. close to one million servings of hash browns.

. over 1.5 million eggs.

. at least 14 million slices of ham.

. more than 22 million slices of pie.

The statistic that really got to Samuels concerned pecans. According to the brochure, 21,000,000 pecans had found their way into the restaurant's waffles, or about 334,000 pounds. That's a lot of pecans.

Satisfied with his breakfast and delighted with his knowledge of Waffle House minutiae, Samuels left a more than modest tip and headed east to Gulf Breeze, where he had a date to speak with the *Dorchester's* radar officer, Lieutenant Aubrey Burch.

Gulf Breeze was located at the western end of the Florida "panhandle," next door to its big cousin, Pensacola. Very much like his beloved San Francisco, the town was located on a peninsula and, therefore, surrounded by bodies of water on three sides, the Gulf of Mexico, Santa Rosa Sound, and Pensacola Bay. To get to Gulf Breeze he had to cross the Pensacola Bay Bridge before motoring along US 98 and the Gulf Islands National Seashore.

Samuels knew little about the town beyond two obscure facts. It had made the news in the late 50's when the local folks, being of sound mind, claimed to have seen "UFO's." The Navy, of course, suggested, however kindly, that people were mistaken. A large weather balloon the Navy's brass said unconvincingly, or possibly a new high-speed jet out of the nearby Pensacola Naval Base, but not UFO's. Beyond that, no aliens were sighted except for the usual influx of college students during the Easter rush to the wide, beautiful beaches, which made the area so lovely. As to alien experiments on earthlings, well that's another story according to some citizens.

As to the other unusual fact... The AAA, the American Automobile Association designated Gulf Breeze a "strict enforcement area" for traffic laws, an honor just short of being labeled a "speed trap." As Samuels drove, he could see why. Police cars were highly visible on US 98, the main drag through the town. To put it mildly, except for tourists, who still thought they were driving in the wide-open spaces of Wyoming or Texas, the locals all puttered along a shade under the designated speed limit. Averse to a ticket for speeding, Samuels drove with a light foot.

Aubrey Burch lived in a gated community off of US 98 and adjacent to the "national seashore." After being checked at the gate by an old guy with bushy gray hair and a straight-as-an-arrow stance, who questioned his visitor intensely, Samuels was finally given the hands' up sign to proceed.

"Who are you here to see?" the guard had demanded.

"Aubrey Burch."

"He's expecting you?"

"Yes."

"I'll check with him."

"Good."

And after a short wait and one phone call ...

"He's home."

"And?"

"You're cleared."

"Thanks."

"Be careful ..."

"Of?"

"The old folks ..."

"Because?"

"Some of them don't see very well ..."

"Really?"

"Or hear..."

"No kidding."

"You wouldn't want to hit one of our senior citizens."

"Of course not."

Burch's home was large and sprawling, a rustic structure of wood and shingles, and large panoramic windows to permit the sun's rays to warm the place, and to give those inside a magnificent view of the water. Local vegetation, enhanced by shady bushes brought in for just that purpose, pointed to a home well landscaped. As it turned out, Burch had majored in floriculture before joining the Navy and he still enjoyed tilling the soil with the aid of his wife.

The home had an expansive back yard without walls, which provided for a generous view of Santa Rosa Sound. A small sailboat, the *Lucky Lady*, was tied up to a wooden pier, more a petite platform, which rose and fell as gentle waves lapped against it. All in all, it was obvious that Burch had found his piece of heaven.

Burch's lovely wife, Mary, met Samuels at the door and ushered him into her home with a pleasing smile and a vigorous handshake.

"You didn't get lost," she exclaimed.

"Almost," Samuels replied.

"Take a load off in the living room. Aubrey been so excited, ever since you wrote him."

"Good to hear."

"He loved the four articles you enclosed, especially the one about the Captain. It really got to him." I read them to him many times."

"Oh?"

Aubrey Burch was sitting in a comfortable Lazy-Boy chair in the living room. He looked up at Samuels entered the room and cocked his head as the reporter approached before extending his hand. That's when Samuels realized the former radar officer was blind.

"Glad you made it," he said.

"My thought, too."

"It's been a long time since I talked to anyone about that night."

"He's had many sleepless nights, though," Mary added. "Lots of bad dreams, you understand."

"I do."

"Tell us again what this is all about," Burch said quizzically.

Samuels gathered himself and then shared his odyssey to date. He left little out."

"Wow," Mary said. "The Kennedys are involved. You know, I cast my vote for him. Such a handsome young man."

"I didn't," Burch announced. "Nixon was my man."

"We split our vote, Mr. Samuels, after some heated discussions."

"Close election," Samuels said.

"Nixon would have won," Burch said defiantly, "if it hadn't been for those dead people voting in Cook County."

"Our political system has its quirks," Samuels uttered, not knowing what else to say to his Nixon fan.

"Amen," Burch said. "Now, how can I help you."

"As I said in my letter, I'm trying to find out if Big Hit, the cook, was the Fifth Chaplain."

Aubrey Burch stared straight ahead and, so it seemed, directly into that night when the world ended, at least temporarily for him.

"I saw a lot of Big Hit. As the chief radar officer, I was locked into a tiny windowless room with banks of electronic instruments, including a large, specially designed speaker system. Four hours in, four hours out, always listening, always afraid to hear something. Big Hit was my buddy. Whenever he could, he would bring me coffee and a smuggled doughnut, always chocolate, my favorite, as I remember. He took care of my assistant, too."

"He brought you your meals, too, didn't he Aubrey?" Mary stated more than asked.

"Absolutely. If he couldn't deliver them himself, Cookie would bring them. They were quite a team. You know they worked for the cruise line before the war, Mr. Samuels."

"Yes, I found that out recently."

"Made great cakes and pies, let me tell you."

"And doughnuts?"

"And doughnuts," Burch said with a beguiling smile.

"He took good care of you."

"He didn't want us to fall asleep at the wheel, so to speak. It was our job to find and locate a U-boat before it attacked us. We were always listening. Always! The black coffee he made, thick as syrup, always jolted my nerves. No way I could drift off with that stuff in me."

"Listening?" Samuels asked.

"We had the latest sonar. The British had developed it and installed it in our ships, even the old *Dorchester*. We were using it for the first time. Sonar --- "**So**und **N**avigation **a**nd **R**anging" system. It wasn't a passive system. We didn't just listen for a sound made by a vessel, especially a German submarine. We had an active system designed to find those damn U-boats."

"Active, meaning?"

"Our system emitted pulses of sound waves. We listened for echoes, sounds coming back to us. We called the outgoing sounds 'beeps.' We sent out a beep every five seconds, about 17,280 beeps every 24-hours."

"It must have been boring, just sitting there, monitoring the equipment."

Burch's face turned angry for a moment, then understanding creased it. He was dealing with a novice, a reporter with good intensions certainly, but still an innocent in the world of kill or be killed on the high seas, or at least in the radar room.

"Anything but, Mr. Samuels. If the beep came back, we were damn scared. We didn't know if the signal had bounced off a school of codfish or the conning tower of a sub? Anything and everything was suspicious and was treated as hostile. We never wanted to hear that returning echo. We didn't know if the target was coming or going, and since it was only accurate between a quarter and half mile, we didn't know how close we were to the enemy. No matter how long we managed the radar, we were always scared to death in that room."

As Burch was talking, Mary had excused herself to see about things in the kitchen. She now returned with a platter of Winchell chocolate doughnuts, and coffee for all.

"Mr. Samuels, help yourself. Do you take cream or sugar?"

"Just as it is, thank you."

"I like your style, Samuels. Black coffee, good man."

"But not as thick as syrup," Mary cried in mock horror.

"Good woman to have around," Burch said. "You married?" he asked.

"Yes."

"Got a good lady?"

"As you do, the best."

Mary handed her husband his plate, and he seemed to know where his coffee was on a small tray next to him.

"Can you tell me anything more about Big Hit?" Samuels asked.

"He made sure I never missed a meal. If I were on duty during mess, he'd bring the food to me and anyone else on duty in the radar room. He always had a kind word, all of which was very reassuring once we got into *Torpedo Junction*."

121

"I've heard of that place," Samuels volunteered.

"Not a place exactly," Burch said. "More a location, south and east of Newfoundland, an area where American submarine reconnaissance didn't exist. Our planes just couldn't cover this area. Not enough fuel for extended flying time. It was where our planes turned around and headed to their home bases. And the Germans knew this. They waited in wolf packs between 51 and 58 degrees longitude, the killing zone. That's where the *U-223* caught up with us."

Samuels knew about the German submarine, which, on its first foray into the North Atlantic, had come across the ill-starred *Dorchester*.

"The Captain followed the lead ship in the convoy. We zigzagged every 30-minutes in this area according to preset coordinates established after we left Saint John's. We also obeyed the rules."

"Rules?"

"Yes, Mr. Samuels. We couldn't break formation for any reason. We couldn't contact any other ship by radio. We couldn't even communicate by battle lantern. We were like ghosts crossing the water, invisible to each other in the freezing rain, which fell at night and coated our ship in an icy mantle. We were alone and anxious, and so close to Greenland when the *U-223* found us."

What could Samuels say? He didn't want to appear callous, but he had to ask the question. "How did you get out of the radar room?"

The old man heard the question, no doubt about that. If a face can relive the past, Aubrey Burch's did, first showing surprise, then comprehension, and finally fear, even has his unseeing eyes stared straight ahead.

"The torpedo tore through the engine room and knock hell out of my little spot. A large, heavy transformer fell over and knocked me sidewise and almost unconscious. The stupid thing hit me in the head and slashed a six-inch cut across my temple. The doctors told me later, it bruised by optic nerve, eventually leaving me blind. As it was, with blood covering my eyes, I couldn't see a thing. Fortunately, Big Hit was in the room. That man carried me through smashed up corridors to the main deck. I wouldn't have made it without his help."

It was obvious Burch was painfully recalling the past. A

tremendous effort was being made on his part to tell what happened. His wife was becoming increasingly concerned as her husband talked. Already in weak health, she didn't want him to tax himself.

"Aubrey, do you want to rest?" she asked. "You can continue later, if you would like."

"No. Let's get this over with. Once on deck, Big Hit could see I couldn't. He tied a rope around my waist, and with the help of his friend, Cookie, they lowered me into the water. Christ, that was so damn cold. It just sucked the breath right out of you. One moment I had been comfortably warm in the radar room, the next moment I'm freezing to death. A moment later, Cookie jumped in and swam with me to a doughnut raft. I never saw Big Hit and Cookie after that."

"Do you think he might have been the "Fifth Chaplain?"

"Why not?" Burch asked. "He conducted himself like one. Jesus, he saved my life at the risk of his own. No chaplain ever acted with greater grace. He's gets my vote."

Samuels was pleased with Burch's answer. The facts, though still very inconclusive, were falling into place.

"Thank you for your help, Mr. Burch."

"You're welcome. But don't leave yet. Mary, get my *Bible*. I need to show something to Mr. Samuels."

In a moment, Mary returned with a well-worn *Bible*. From it, she extracted a tired piece of paper with ink smeared cursive writing.

"Do you want me to read it, dear?" she asked her husband.

"No, just hand it to Mr. Samuels. I know it by heart."

Amazingly, he did.

Holy Father, we come before you in crisis. We are driven down by our enemies and look to you as David looked when his enemies threatened to destroy him. We are powerless to save ourselves and pray that you will bless and preserve us. In the name of the Father, the Son, and the Holy Ghost, amen.

"Father Washington made that prayer," Burch said, "the night before we were torpedoed. It was such a beautiful prayer. I wrote it down as best I could. It was lost, of course, after the *Dorchester* was hit, but I kept hearing it in the hospital. It just wouldn't go away.

Think of that, long after the good priest died, he was still alive in my mind."

Samuels was at a loss for words. Indeed, the prayer was beautiful, something that would be shared with his readers.

"Mr. Samuels, you do right by him. When the enemy threatened to destroy me, and I felt so powerless, God sent this man of peace to save me. In my mind, Big Hit is your 'Fifth Chaplain.' Make no mistake about that."

CHAPTER 16

THE CHASE

LATE APRIL – SAN FRANCISCO

It was nice to be home. One doesn't appreciate his own bed and clean sheets until he camps out in motels, one day after another. Keeping this in mind, Robert Samuels was glad to leave the Deep South. As he reminded himself, he was a "fog" man unused to and discomforted by high humidity and a blazing sun, which left you with shirts clinging to your skin and your throat panting for a cold drink. San Francisco, by and large was different, sweaters and a steaming cup of coffee were the coin of this realm.

Samuels was satisfied with trip to the South. He had learned a lot about Big Hit and was now convinced, based on the evidence collected to this point, that the cook was without question the "Fifth Chaplain." True, there was no "smoking gun" to prove beyond any doubt that Morris Jones was the missing chaplain. But the reverse was also true. There was no proof he wasn't.

In his summary report to Kurtz and the Attorney-General, he had stated the case matter-of-factly:

Morris Jones had: (1) saved the life of the radar officer after the U-223 struck; (2) assisted the Captain on the main deck in handing out life jackets; (3) given away his own life jacket; remained in the proximity of the Chaplains as the ship was sinking; and (4) displayed a self-sacrificing behavior.

For Samuels, the difficult quest for the "Fifth Chaplain" was over.

When asked by Kurtz, what he intended to do now, Samuels was equally succinct. He wanted to visit the relatives of the Chaplains and, if possible, travel to Europe to interview any surviving members of the *U-223*. When asked why, he told Kurtz he needed to more fully understand the essence of men who would willingly sacrifice themselves for others. As for the Germans, he needed to find out how they felt about the events of almost 20-years ago.

Samuels also pointed out that, as in the case of the radar officer, he would submit human-interest stories to the *Chronicle* as they related to the Four Chaplains. Kurtz, after some quiet soul searching, accepted this, believing that public interest warranty further episodes. It was also good politics from his point of view. With the President aboard and the Attorney-General pleased, Samuels was given the green light.

It was nice being home with the kids again. In just a short time, Matt seemed to spurt upward, while Rachel was maturing into an elegant, charming senior in high school. Talk about college was definitely in the air. And, of course, it was nice to have a home made meal again, the Waffle House notwithstanding. It was pleasant to again take an evening walk with his wife, to enjoy her company, and to share with her his thoughts about Big-Hit.

The Source had read Samuels' report. He was anything but pleased as he dialed the phone.

"Stretch, it's me."

"Okay."

"It's time to turn Baldy loose."

"Where?"

"San Francisco."

"How hard?"

"Enough to get him to stop his research."

"Baldy will be most pleased."

Samuels' report had also upset the Director of the FBI.

"I don't want a Negro on any God damn stamp!" he had screamed to an aide. "It's un-American."

"Sir ..."

"That's all we need," the furious law enforcer continued, "more of those self-righteous college kids pouring into the South to campaign for a cook."

"Perhaps..."

"What the hell is the country coming to?" the Director stammered."

"But..."

"Get me Brady and Hill on the phone. It's time to push back. I'll be damned if I'll let the Kennedy use this Big Hit to pass their civil rights legislation."

"What did the Director say?" Hill asked in a faint voice.

"It's push back time," Brady said.

"Muscles or threats?"

"Threats --- IRS review of his taxes, past associations with liberal groups, and possibly conspiring to incite domestic violence for openers."

"Jesus."

"If that doesn't work, we'll talk about governments loans and grants for college."

"Cheap shot at his kids," Hill said. "Any other gems?"

"Pressure on his newspaper."

"Are we really going to do this? Hill asked.

"You still dislike Alaska?"

"Hate the cold."

"Well, that's why we're going to follow orders.

Much later and unaware of all this, Robert Samuels, on the advice of his wife, was preparing to jog in Mountain Lake Park.

"You'll enjoy the exercise. Give your brain a chance to rest."

"Okay, boss."

"Got your good running shoes, Robert? Lynn asked.

"Not the old Converse?"

"The new ones I bought you from Stretchers."

"Oh."

"Oh, what?"

"I'm wearing them."

"Good. Got your water bottle, the nice metal one the kids got you?"

"Belted."

"Power bar?"

"In my sweatshirt pocket."

"Well then, you're ready for anything."

With that and a kiss, Samuels drove across town to Mountain Lake Park, a lovely recreational area in the Outer Richmond area between 6th Avenue and 11th Avenue above Lake Street. Once a city reservoir, the lake now played host to various kinds of ducks and tall, very green tule stalks growing in marsh-like soil. Near the lake were tennis courts, two meadows for impromptu games of football and baseball by the younger set, and a children's area complete with slides, swings, and the much in demand sand boxes.

Around the entire park ran a wide path to accommodate bike riders, joggers, walkers, moms with strollers, dogs on leashes, and kids who had escaped from their parent's grip. Somehow they all got along. Along the path the city had constructed special exercise spots, where anyone could do chin lifts (or try to), squats, push-ups (no one really counted), rope climbing, or just use the exercise bars in some exotic way. For some, the spots were just a place to rest.

Samuels found himself enjoying his jog through the early morning fog, which cooled him as ran at a leisurely pace along the path. He felt energized. He felt good. It was so nice to be away from airports and mad dashes to make his flight, and later to find his luggage adrift in a world of look-a-like suitcases. At least for a moment, he didn't have to worry about car rentals, hotel reservations, and appointments to keep. And most of all, having completed his latest story for the *Chronicle*, there was no pressure to finish another article.

In short, Samuels was feeling no stress. He realized, of course, that this couldn't last. And it wouldn't.

He was running past a small meadow bordering 7th Avenue, when he saw the two men again. Samuels had seen them earlier, running together, always staying about twenty-five yards behind him. At first he had felt no concern. The park was open to everyone. But now, as he looked back, it seemed like this tandem was gaining on him. One was husky and quite bald. The other was slight in build and struggling, it seemed, to keep up. For no good reason, a little bell began sounding deep within Samuels' unconscious, reminding him to be wary. But, of what, he thought?

Samuels decide to test the vibes he was getting. He cut across the small meadow and plowed into the "monkey trees," a dense area of heavy foliage and spindly trees. He plunged deeper into this thicket. As a kid, he had played "war" here with his boyhood friends. He knew the area by heart. He stopped to catch his breath and to listen. He heard nothing. After a few minutes, he figured it was just his imagination running a little wild. He quietly left his cover and reentered the meadow.

Less than ten yards away, he saw the two men. They were staring at him. The little bell was ringing more insistently now. Samuels took off, running all out in a furious sprint to lose the two men.

They followed, slipping into a higher gear, and charging after him. The chase was on.

Samuels blew past other joggers and, of course, the walkers.

He headed toward "old man's land," as he called it. The city had built a three-sided building in the park, where people could play chess and checkers, and occasionally, cards. It was frequent by older, retired guys.

Pulling around a turn, Samuels reached his destination, slowed, and nonchalantly milled around with the "elders," even as he sought to catch his breath.

"Hey, kid, want to play a game of checker?" one bearded fellow asked.

"Just watching."

"You okay?" a gravely voiced fellow asked.

"Sure. Just been running hard."

Samuels watched as the two men ran past. Fooled them, Samuels thought. A moment later, the two returned. Standing with hands on their hips and breathing hard, they checked out the senior citizens. To the extent he could, Samuels tried to hide himself among the players by sitting and feinted interest in a hotly contested chess match.

After a few minutes, he risked running again, and seeing no one, took off toward the lake. Almost immediately, the two men chasing him appeared, seemingly out of nowhere, and ran after him. For Samuels, there was no longer any need for the bell to toll. His "fight or flight" juices kicked in. He ran like hell.

As he neared the lake, memories from childhood emerged. He had hidden, as a kid, in the tall groves of tules, green stalks which rose higher than a man's head. It had been a great place to elude his buddies. Could he do it again? There was no need to debate the issue. With his feet sticking in the marsh-like sand, Samuels slithered into this escapist world of childhood. Walking carefully, but quickly, he maneuvered his way through the bog. Certainly, no one could follow him here. Right? Or could they?

After hiding for about twenty minutes, Samuels slunk out of the tules. Though he was scratched, seemingly everywhere by the blade shaped stalks, he felt pretty good. He had lost the bad guys. Of course, his new Stretchers were waterlogged and discolored. Still he was feeling victorious. Not even the mud clinging to his legs and up to the knees could disavow his happiness. His childhood world had saved him. He had won.

Samuels stepped out into the open. He was next to the children's play area and the tennis courts. Happily, lots of moms were with their kids, and the three courts were full of players.

Then he saw them.

Somehow the two men had predicted his flight. With nasty smiles, they were waiting for him.

Who were these guys? Samuels asked himself. What do they want? Are they really dangerous?

Samuels' feet answered the questions. As if own their volition, they took off, dragging him along at a sprinter's speed. His pursuers flew after him.

Samuels flew by mothers swinging their kids and poorly hit tennis balls flying through the air. Ahead was the big meadow, where he hoped to finally lose these guys.

In Samuels' head he was thinking about *Terry and the Pirates*, and how they would get out of this jam. The *Phantom* came to mind, but Samuels didn't have a skeleton ring or a great white stallion to leap upon. His beloved *Green Hornet* struggled for his attention, but for what purpose? Samuels didn't have the power of his favorite boyhood comic strips.

Running alone at breakneck speed, Samuels didn't notice the raised sprinkler head. But it noticed him. In one terrible lapse of attention, he tripped and fell hard onto the wet grass, and before he could move Baldy pounced on him. He felt the wind knocked out of him. He heard his assailant yell, "Grab his arms, Nails." In a moment he was pinned to the turf like a trout out of the water and ready to be filleted. What could he do? The more he struggled, Baldy, who felt like a bowling ball, pressed down on him.

Samuels knew he was getting dizzy. With Baldy on him, he could hardly breathe. It was his worst nightmare, choking to death. Nausea began to over take him. He tasted bile in his mouth. For the first time, real fear saturated his mind. He was scared to death.

"What do you guys want? Samuels screamed. "Take my wallet," he continued, "if you want."

"We don't want your money," Nails said with obvious glee.

"What, then?"

"We're here to give you some advice," Baldy spat out at Samuels. "Pay attention."

"Advice?" Samuels grunted.

"Give up the quest," Baldy said with a hiss.

"The what?"

"Don't quest me, jerk," Baldy said as he smacked Samuels across the face. "Stop looking for the "Fifth Chaplain.""

"What are you talking about?" Samuels asked through clenched teeth.

"And no more articles in the *Chronicle*," Nails oozed as again Baldy slapped Samuels across the face.

Samuels felt humiliated. It was one thing to be chased and tackled by two guys, but another to be slapped silly. Somehow he felt humiliated by the slaps. A punch in the face by a hard fist, okay. Kicked in the groin not fun, but somehow okay. But a slap, that was something entirely unfair, unmanly, and unfair.

He felt powerless, the way he had on the *Ward* when the kamikaze plane bore in and death stared him in the face. He remembered screaming at the plane, "Stay away from my ship," and then the Zero blew up literally in his face.

At that moment something snapped in Samuels. Fear and anger collided in his mind, and he was overwhelmed with rage. He went a little crazy.

Wiggling his arm, he freed one hand and found what pure instinct was directing him to do. He fingered the metal water bottle, clasped it tightly and swung it with all his might at Baldy. He caught his oppressor by surprise. Filled with water, the bottle crashed into Baldy's surprised face, leaving a large, nasty cut near his eye and, hopefully, a big purple bruise in time. Caught off guard by the painful attack, Baldy released him. Pushed by a surge of adrenaline,

Samuels leaped to his feet, and without thinking, he kicked Baldy in the groin, which brought the man to his knees yelling in pain.

Then Samuels turned to Nails and leaped upon him, screaming as he did so, as had his ancestors 10,000 years ago before case law and social mores against violence. Fear was gone. Hesitation was gone. Only anger remained, pure and unadulterated, a living force that needed to be satiated. Samuels wanted to hurt someone. The rage was all consuming. He barreled into the thin man, slamming him to the ground with a resounding thud. He then hit him again and again, breaking his nose, and loosening a few teeth, and enjoying every moment of it on some level beyond his understanding.

The taste of the jungle was in Samuels' mouth. The trappings of a civilized man were gone, replaced by a primeval creature, a savage with blood lust in his eyes. He had metamorphosed into a killer. Turning back to Baldy, he reared back and with untamed fury kicked him in the face. Samuels heard a crunching sound and felt good about it.

He was about to deliver another roundhouse kick when two men ran up to him yelling, "That's enough, tough guy." Fists clenched and tight-lipped, Samuels prepared to take on the two men. He was not yet out of the jungle.

Then he saw it, a badge held high, and heard a sharp voice say, "FBI."

CHAPTER 17

RECOVERY

LATE APRIL – SAN FRANCISCO

The nice, sage-like doctor from the V.A. Hospital had gone. He had given Robert Samuels a complete check. He found no lasting damage. A dab of antibiotic cream and clean gauze bandages took care of most everything. No stitches were needed. A bloody face had hid no major cuts, only minor bruises. No bones were broken. The doctor left recommending the oldest advice: "Get some rest." And, as he was leaving the house, he added, "Try to avoid further confrontations for awhile."

Samuels was more than happy to oblige the doctor's advice. He was sore and bone weary, and still shocked at what had occurred.

To his family and the two FBI agents gathered in his living room an hour later he said, "I still can't believe what happened."

"Believe it," said Brady. 'You really mixed it up today."

"With two KKK members," Hill added.

"Pretty tough guys, according to their records," Brady suggested.

"Where are they now?" Lynn asked.

"In custody," Hill said flatly. "Still being treated by the medics. Your husband did a number on them. Here, check this photograph."

Lynn looked. As did the kids… Two bloodied faces stared back at them. It looked like they had been in a train wreck. Matt was the first to respond, "Go, Dad."

"My husband did this?" Lynn asked.

"Dad, I thought you were a pacifist. That violence was unjustifiable."

Samuels kept his peace. What could he say? He glanced over at Kieran, who was just staring at him with a "wow" look on his face.

"What will happen to them?" Rachel asked sourly.

"Bail or jail until a hearing," Brady replied. "Mr. Samuels has already pressed charges."

"Doesn't sound like much," Rachel countered.

"Up to the judge," Hill told her.

Matt, who was looking at his father with newly found pride, said, "Dad, you're so cool. Wait until my friends hear all about this."

"Let's not advertise too much," Lynn volunteered.

"No need to worry about that, Mrs. Samuels," Hill said casually. "The *Chronicle* already has the story. The morning edition, pictures and all, will tell all."

"Dad, you could be on television," Matt said with glee. "KRON will want to interview you, I bet."

"Well, not today, that's for sure," Samuels quickly said. "I need to get some rest."

Reluctantly, Hill said, "Perhaps we could go over things just one more time for the record."

"Just to make sure you've covered everything," Brady added.

And so Samuels did.

As he did, the kids noticed actual physical changes in their father. First, his fists close, opened, and then clenched tightly. His face, at first pleasant looking, began to reshape itself. They saw surprise, then anger, and finally, rage as his face contorted. The muscles of his body tightened and his breathing became shallow and forced. His voice turned harsh, almost guttural. For the kids, it was like watching Dr. Jekyll turn into Mr. Hyde. To tell the truth, the transformation scared them.

"Are you okay?" Rachel asked her father.

"Dad, this is frightening," Matt wailed.

Samuels finished his retelling of the day's events at the park, and slowly the contortions reversed themselves. In short order, he was good old dad again and the tensions dissipated.

"What did I marry," Lynn asked, "a super agent?"

"No. I'm a man of peace given to passivity whenever possible," Samuels responded with a thin smile. "I wouldn't hurt an ant."

At that the two agents uttered in disbelief, "We guess it wasn't possible today, right Mr. Samuels?"

It was Kieran, though, who asked the key question. "Uncle Bob, will these KKK guys try this again?"

If others were impressed with Samuels' actions, this certainly was not the case in the Director's Office.

"Where the hell were our guys when all this went down?" Hoover asked an aide sharply.

"They lost Samuels in the park," the aide said haltingly.

"Christ, how could they lose him?"

"Hill and Brady didn't say in their report."

"What's the medical report on Samuels?"

"Bruised but nothing broken," the aide said a bit too calmly.

"And the two he fought with?"

"In custody."

"Background?"

"KKK," the aide said nervously. "From the South, Tennessee."

"Jesus Christ, the media will make a hero out of Samuels, and that damn Big Hit guy."

"It would seem so," the aide whispered.

"What?"

"Nothing, sir. Any orders for Brady and Hill?"

"Stay close to Samuels."

"Yes sir."

"Damn. This can only help the Kennedys," the Director spat out. "This was the last thing I needed."

The mood was different in the Justice Building. At first the Attorney-General had been furious, bellowing, "Where was the FBI backup, Kurtz?"

"It seems they lost our reporter."

"I don't believe it."

"It's in their report, sir," Kurtz said calmly.

The nervous Robert Kennedy sprung to his feet and began to laugh, asking, "Samuels really kicked their ass?"

"It appears so."

"Son-of-a-bitch, we've got a tiger on the payroll."

"He seems to have surprised everyone," Kurtz quipped.

"Are you sure he's Jewish and not Irish?" Kennedy asked.

"Both. His father was born in Dublin."

"That cuts it. No more slip-ups. I need to keep this guy healthy."

"For the Irish?" Kurtz asked.

"For the Irish," Kennedy confirmed.

In another part of the Justice Department, the Source sat quietly, and very unhappily. Privy to the FBI report, he was furious with Baldy and Nails for botching what should have been an easy deal, just scare the crap out of the guy. Now his KKK brothers were languishing in jail. Botching was one thing, but getting beat up in the process by a reporter, well that was too much. Hell, now the FBI would have no choice but to intensify their supervision of Samuels. It would be difficult to get close to Samuels again.

It was time to call Stretch with the "good news," the Source thought sarcastically. It was time to lay low for a while. But first things first, bail would have to be arranged for Baldy and Nails.

After reviewing everything with Samuels, Brady and Hill left and headed for O'Doul's Steak House in the financial district.

"You'll like the food," Hill pointed out to his partner. "Great steaks. Excellent sandwiches."

"Beer?"

"Foreign and domestic, larger and ale, whatever you want."

As Hill drove in the tight San Francisco traffic, they discussed what was on their minds. Brady began, saying, "Hoover can go and screw himself."

"The Director will freak," Hill replied, "if I'm thinking what you're thinking."

"Samuels won't be intimated by us, no matter what pressure we put on his kids or the newspaper."

"I saw it in his eyes, Brady. He's a warrior. Hell, he stared down a Jap kamikaze."

"He sure beat the crap out of those guys."

"One things, though," Brady said.

"Yeah?"

"How did Baldy and Nails know about Samuels?"

The two men sat quietly as they moved into the downtown area and found a place to park, an almost unheard of occurrence in San Francisco.

"Two dollars per hour to park... What a rip off" Brady said.

"You'll enjoy the steak," Hill reminded him. "Stop complaining."

"Before we eat," Brady said, "we still have an open question."

"Inside information."

"A source in the Justice Department? Brady asked.

"Possibly. We can't rule out our own department."

"We need to find this mole."

"We need an outside, inside man, Hill explained.

"Harry. Do you think Harry would do it?"

"He's retired and he knows the Bureau," Hill told Brady.

"And he hates Hoover's ass," Brady said with a laugh.

"Which is what we need in this situation."

"Amen, brother," Brady said. Let's eat. We'll call him later."

That night, as Samuels was about to fall asleep, Lynn turned to him and said, "It's true, a wife never really know your husband."

"You know me."

"Do I?"

"You know I love you and the kids."

"True. But who was that other guy?"

"Someone who got all bruised up."

"You're sore, dear?"

"Everywhere."

"Would a kiss help?"

"Couldn't hurt, could it?"

"Let's see."

CHAPTER 18

RESEARCH

JUNE – SAN FRANCISCO

"We're ready" Rachel said with excitement in her voice. "Let's get started."

"Okay," Robert Samuels said. "How about your brother?"

"Present and accounted for," Matt piped. "I'm more than ready, too."

"Where's mom?" Rachel asked.

"Coming, kids, let's do it."

Weeks ago the kids, led by Rachel, placed a simple proposition before their father. "We want to help with your research."

"What do you have in mind?"

"We, Matt and I, want to learn about the Four Chaplains," she said. "It would be a great topic for our school research paper, and it would help you."

"What'd say, dad?" Matt asked.

What could Samuels say? His kids were bursting at the seams in their desire to help him. Still, he moved cautiously. "Lynn, what do you think?" he asked.

"It would make for a great family project."

"So?"

"The family that researches together stays together," she said

140

with a glow. "And it would make up for the time you've been away from home."

"I'll take that as an affirmative vote."

"Absolutely."

Outwardly, Samuels seemed to give in grudgingly. Inwardly, he was tickled. He was delighted the kids wanted to put aside the teen-age addiction to the latest music, movie, or clothing fad for this project.

"You're sure you want to do this?" Samuels asked the kids. "You're taking on a big task."

"Dad," Rachel said convincing," we've talked about it with mom. We can do this."

"I'm the last to know," Samuels wailed. "This smells of a conspiracy."

"Just getting our ducks in line," Matt said, as he quoted one of Samuels' favorite lines."

"Okay, you're on. I'll give you what information I have and you do the rest. And another thing, I expect you to keep up your school grades and get an "A" from your teachers for this research."

The kids smiled and nodded in agreement. Rachel flew to her dad and gave him a 100% happiness kiss. Matt sauntered over and bumped chests with his father the way professional football players did after a winning score. It was a guy thing. Kieran extended a hand and was surprised when Samuels added a big hug. For her part, Lynn merely nodded in approval with a twinkle in her eyes.

A deal was struck. For weeks the kids hit both their schoolbooks and the information provided by Samuels. They also lived in the local public library and then the two big time ones where they felt quite grown up, the library at San Francisco State, and the queen library at Berkley across the bay at CAL. In addition, they pursued information from the Defense Department, and especially the Navy with the help of Samuels.

The big day finally arrived when they would share their information. Now it was time to see what they had learned. "You're up, Rachel." Samuels said. "It's time to get this show on the road."

Samuels pushed Kurtz to be present. He also invited his FBI shadows, Brady and Hill, to hear what the kids had learned. Surprisingly, they all agreed to be present. Lynn welcomed them to the living room, where she plied them with chips and dips, and cold beer for the men, and soft drinks for the kids. The FBI agents considered the occasion as a non-work moment and enjoyed cold one.

Samuels introduced his kids on the big day, pointing out they had divided the presentation task into two parts. Rachel would first talk about George Fox and Clark Poling. Matt would follow up and present information about Alex Goode and John Washington.

A little anxious before this adult group, Rachel hesitated before opening her notebook. Gripping the little podium nicely balanced on a small table, which Samuels had provided for the kids, she began in a halting voice, which grew stronger as she spoke.

RACHEL

"The Four Chaplains first met at Harvard University, where the Army trained them for their chaplain's duties in wartime. They were all called by their faith to serve their God by ministering to those in the service. They were also very patriotic. They wanted to help their country. They were part of over 9,000 chaplains, who served during World War II."

Wow," thought Samuels, my little girl has turned into a real scholar.

"The Four Chaplains were all lieutenants. My first chaplain, George Fox, was the oldest. He was 42-years old. He was the only one of the four who had already been in a war. He had lied about his age in order to enlist in World War I. He was a medical assistant during the conflict, and he earned the Silver Star for bravery under fire when he helped wounded soldiers. He also received a Purple Heart for his own injuries, which occurred one day before the Armistice. After leaving the Army, he went back to school and eventually became a Methodist minister in 1934. He attended the seminary at Boston University and was later a pastor in small Vermont communities. Later he married Isadora, and they had two children, Wyatt and

Mary Louise. After Pearl Harbor, Reverend Fox was torn between his duty to his family, his congregation, and his country. Looking up from her notes, Rachel said, "I think Reverend Fox was on to something here. His belief caused him to reenlist. He was under no legal obligation to do so."

Both Samuels and Lynn were impressed with their daughter's presentation and what came next.

"Reverend Fox really knew something about war. He saw the wounded in France, like something from a nightmare with faces blown away, arms and legs shredded and mangled. He heard the agonized and painful screams of men with gangrene. He smelled death on the Western front. It was a constant presence. I think it's remarkable he was willing to go back to all that."

"My second chaplain was Clark Poling, Jr. His father had been a Chaplain in World War I. The younger Poling was thirty years old when he enlisted in the Army. He was the youngest of the Chaplains. He studied at the Yale University Divinity School and was ordained in the Dutch Reform church and was a pastor in Schenectady, New York. His father, who had been a Chaplain in the First World War, told him that Chaplains had the highest mortality rate among soldiers. That didn't stop the younger Polling. He still signed up and was accepted by the Army.

"He told his dad not to pray for him, pointing out that wouldn't be fair because many will not return. He asked his father to pray that he would be adequate, that he would do his job with distinction. Poling was torn between peace and war. He wondered how could a man of peace kill? But on the other hand, how could a man of faith refuse to defend the freedom God had so graciously provided? According to his family, he made this prayer at his last Christmas together, December 1942:

Thank you, God, for our freedom. Help us to rise to the challenge we face today in protecting it. Help us have the courage, in your name, to do what is necessary to defend our nation and our families from evil.

Without question, Samuels felt immense pride as he listened to his daughter speak. She was smart and she was beautiful. Glancing over at Lynn, who was absolutely glowing in pride, he winked approval as Rachel finished.

The guests seemed equally taken by Rachel's remarks. Kurtz, the serious bureaucrat, and a bit of a curmudgeon, seemed more like a grandfather today, displaying a "Aren't my grandkids terrific?" look on his face. As for my FBI buddies, they appeared charmed by the youngsters. No question, they were fast becoming Uncle Hill and Uncle Brady.

"Well done, Rachel," he said. "Excellent start."

"Thanks, dad. Now its Matt's turn."

Younger that his sister, and sometimes a bit immature, Matt was a big question mark for Samuels. Would he be able to handle this? Samuels shouldn't have been concerned. Matt winked at this mom and started.

MATT

"I researched Father John Washington and Rabbi Alexander Goode. Mom really helped. Some of this was really difficult for me. It still is. I'll start with Father Washington.

"He was one of seven children of Irish immigrants. As a kid, he carried newspapers to help support his family. He wore glasses and loved music. People considered him a tough guy because he led a street gang in New Jersey. He got into all kinds of scrapes with the law before he turned his life around. He attended Seton Hall University and did well in the seminary program. He also developed a fine talent for singing and piano playing.

"His mother, Mary Washington, didn't want him to enlist after Pearl Harbor. She had already lost two sons, Francis, an Army Air Force bombardier, and Leo who was in the Army. She didn't want to lose a third son. Her son, however, had different ideas. He would enlist, but there was a problem. John Washington had poor eyesight. To pass his medical review, he fudged a bit, covering his bad eye twice in order to pass the test. Cheating in this case was, of course, a good thing because he was going to help other men. I guess that's called rationalization."

"I was really impressed by the goals he set for himself as a man. He wanted to conform himself as much as he was able to the example of Christ. He also wanted to acquire the knowledge and strength of will to understand and follow in the steps of Christ. He wanted to live a Christ-like life. As you can imagine, I needed lots of help from mom to understand what this was all about."

"Rabbi Alexander Goode grew up in Brooklyn and earned a doctorate degree from Johns Hopkins University in Middle Eastern languages. He married Theresa Fox, who happened to be a niece of Al Jolson, the famous entertainer. He was ordained from Hebrew University in 1937, when he also gave his first sermon at Temple Beth Israel. In January 1941 he applied to the US Navy. He wanted to be chaplain to seaman. He was turned down. After Pearl Harbor, he applied again and was finally accepted by the Army.

"Goode had a deep interest in interfaith relationships. He believed that the more people knew about one another, the more understanding and compassionate they would be toward people who were different from them. He believed that knowledge and truth made fear and prejudice melt *away*. I think that's cool."

"Good job, Matt," Samuels said with relish. "I'm very pleased by your research and what you've said."

"My sentiments, too," said Kurtz, who was obviously moved by the presentations. "Excellent job."

"We concur," added Hill and Brady, smiling as only prospective uncles can.

"Matt and I," Rachel said, "will continue now with additional information we found through our research. There's a lot more to know about these Chaplains. First of all, we would like to point out what you already know. These four men of different faith gave away their only means of saving themselves in order to save others. It was reported that men rowing away from the *Dorchester* saw the Chaplains clinging to each other on the slanting deck. Their arms were linked together and their heads were bowed as they prayed to the one God whom each of them loved and served. They were amazing men."

Lynn was beaming. Her two wonderful children had come through in a way she had not anticipated. Not only did they provide factual information on an intellectual level but more than that, they comprehended the importance of what they had learned. Her kids were growing up. And what fine role models they now had in their lives.

CHAPTER 19

HARRY

LATE MAY – ARLINGTON, VIRGINIA

Harry Brownstein didn't look like a spy, at least like those in the mold of 007, the British superhero, who defended Western civilization against an assortment of evil geniuses and rogue governments. Brownstein was more like Ian Fleming, a nondescript person of average height and weight with no scars or swagger to draw attention to him. Light brown was his favorite color, perhaps because his eyes were this color, as well as his hair, and, of course, all his suits. He dressed conservatively with modestly priced clothes off the racks. He never raised his voice. He never challenged anyone in a crowded room. He never fed his ego, at least in public. He was in every way, "Mr. Average."

People couldn't remember if they had seen him. If they saw him, they couldn't remember what he looked like. If they talked with him, they couldn't remember the topic of conversation, or if he had even said anything. He was the kind of guy, who, if he stood in front of a large brown-colored house, would disappear.

He was in so many ways the most visible invisible man in the world. Like water in your hands, he slipped through your fingers leaving nary a trace.

And he was the retired FBI agent Hill and Brady had unleashed to locate the source of the leaks concerning Robert Samuels.

Harry was the perfect man for the job. He knew all about the inside of the Justice Department, as well as the FBI. He knew the people. He knew the policies and protocols underlying the cultures of the Bureau, his former employer. In short, he knew how things worked. And it didn't hurt that Harry disliked Hoover.

He had problems with the FBI Director. First and foremost, he absolutely refused to treat the civil rights movement as a potential domestic threat, a form of homebred terrorism. Second, he did not see the college kids riding South, or a Negro minister from Atlanta as a front for the "Reds," that is, for the international Communist movement. Third, while he was willing to use strong-arm tactics with mobsters, thugs, and "commies," he was repulsed when the Bureau catered to such activities against fellow Americans because of their stance on civil liberties.

Harry's problem was that he really did believe in the Constitution. He took the Bill of Rights seriously. He was suspicious of and resistant to any effort by government to curtail them. That stated, he was one of the few members of the FBI, who belonged to the ACLU, the American Civil Liberties Union, which struggled in courtrooms to protect the constitutional liberties and freedoms of citizens. For Hoover, this made him a card-carrying "leftist" and somewhat "pink." And being Jewish didn't help.

Harry's saving grace was simple. He was extraordinarily good at his job. He located "red cells." He infiltrated the mob. He located the dirty Congressional laundry. He had an instinct for fathoming out the bad guys. Thus, Hoover needed his Jewish agent.

Though Harry had a sterling record during the war, having hounded Nazi sympathizers and jailing members of the American Bund movement, it was never enough for the Director, who wanted unquestioned loyalty. Given that, while Harry sought out and uncovered spies for Berlin, Rome, and Tokyo on both coasts in a most resourceful manner, few promotions or awards came his way.

An early retirement and a healthy bonus for his pension proved persuasive in getting Harry to leave the Bureau. Harry was not happy or sad about this. He was driven by one all-embracing passion:

someday he would have, if he was lucky, the opportunity to even the score with the Director.

It seemed that Brady and Hill had provided that opportunity. And he was free to take advantage of it. Harry's wife of thirty years had recently passed away. Cancer was the culprit. His three children, somewhat estranged from him, were long raised and gone, engaging in their own successful professional lives.

Harry was alone. There was no other drag on his time. Harry happily took the job. But not just to get at Hoover, or to nail the spy. Harry had read Samuels' articles in the *Chronicle* once they were syndicated. He was sympathetic. Doing the job was one thing. Having a good justification was another. Protecting Samuels was all he needed for motivation.

He approached the challenge methodically. First, he read all the documents related to the case as supplied by Hill and Brady. Second, he double- checked the background on Baldy and Nails. It wasn't long before he connected the two men to Stretch, who had set bail for them. Third, it didn't any time at all to establish their membership in the KKK. Fourth, intuitively he reasoned there was a connection between the three men and someone in the Justice Department, who had access to the Samuels' case. Fifth, a quiet search of Robert Kennedy's aides suggested only one candidate for "leaker of the year."

Once he zeroed in on Mr. Henry Fairfield, he devoted all his time and energy to establishing a case against this informant, this domestic subversive, who was always a step ahead of Samuels. But that would soon end.

Almost immediately, Harry realized that the Fairfield was his mirror image, an average guy to whom little attention was given, but who was privy to the most sensitive issues. Reining in this guy was like wrestling with his own shadow. Harry felt like he was chasing himself.

As he built an airtight case over the ensuing weeks, the question was what to do with Mr. Fairfield arose. There was, of course, the legal avenue, but that would lead to a lot of embarrassment for the Justice Department. And possibly the White House. Knowing how

Hoover felt about the civil rights movement, little was to be gained going to the Bureau. What, then, was left?

Harry had, when necessary, eliminated problems before in the quiet of the night when all other options failed. Members of the Sicilian mob, who had worked with El Duce against the interests of the United States, had been lost at sea after running afoul of Harry. When he tracked German spies, who tried to infiltrate the defense industry with hopes of sabotage, they simply disappeared. Known Communist agitators had run into brick walls. Leaders of lynch mobs had car accidents on curving roads. Politicians with too many hands in the till received visits from Harry. Quiet talks ensued. Things changed.

As Harry considered the problem of Mr. Fairfield, he did not eliminate any possibility. Instinctively, he knew there would be a day of reckoning.

Mr. Fairfield was already a marked man.

CHAPTER 20

THE WIVES – ISADORE FOX AND MARY WASHINGTON

EARLY AUGUST 1943 – SAN FRANCISCO

Lynn had come up with the idea "Why not focus on the women?" she asked her husband. "I'm sure they could tell you a great deal about their spouses, those special, wonderful men who sacrificed so much."

"Tell the story from their point-of-view?" Samuels asked.

"Yes. And one more thing…"

"And that is…?"

"Don't wait for your book. Write it now for the *Chronicle*, maybe as a series. People are already interested in the story of the Chaplains. A series will spark even more readers. What do you say?"

"I always agree with you, Lynn, especially when you have the better argument."

Over the next two months, by phone, mail, and in person, Samuels communicated with the wives and relatives of the Four Chaplains. His research was exacting and complete to the extent information was shared by the women. Often he took Lynn with him or Rachel when interviewing surviving spouses, relatives, and friends. The presence of a woman seemed to help. He did so with the full support of Kurtz, and with the "backup" of his children's newly acquired uncles, who discretely tagged along. Politically speaking, the White

House saw this as a terrific way to prepare the public for the looming civil rights legislation. The vote of women was important. As for his editor at the paper, he couldn't wait to run the series.

Surprisingly, Samuels began his series with a prologue about a man, one Colonel Frederick Gillespie and a story defying belief.

In 1943, Gillespie worked in the New York port of embarkation. His headquarters was in Brooklyn. It was his job to determine what men went on what ships in order to bring order to the convoy, and to make sure the right men with the right skills were transported to where they were most needed. As head of personnel at the command center, he was responsible for all troopships heading to Europe.

It was a big job. No computers, just pencil and paper and an excellent staff. Somehow Gillespie got the job done.

It was also a disheartening job. Frustration prevailed in his office. The reason for this was simple. A convoy plan would be drawn up. Crews for the ships determined. Cargo allocated for each ship: trucks, jeeps, tanks, guns, ammo, food, landing crafts, and black oil, everything needed to make war. And then there would be changes. And some at the last possible moment before ships would leave for Saint John's, Canada, forcing the Colonel to make decisions on the run.

True to form Gillespie had a problem. Two chaplains were scratched from the *USAT Dorchester*. Two replacement chaplains were needed, a second Protestant and a Catholic priest. The Colonel scanned a long list of names, all Chaplains, which was at his command. He plucked two names out, John Washington and Clark Poling. Messages were sent to both men, as earlier messages had been sent to George Fox and Alexander Goode.

You are hereby ordered to report to Camp Myles Standish,
    Taunton, Massachusetts, for special assignment
0700 HRS
    3 January 1943. This is a classification order under the authority of the Secretary of War.

Both Washington and Poling had won Gillespie's private lottery. Ironically, both men, though accepted by the military and trained to be combat chaplains, were posted to safe U.S bases, where they thought they would fight the war under personal duress. They wanted to be where the action was, where the men were fighting, not safely hidden away in the States. Gillespie had now changed their personal histories. Two chaplains had been scratched from his original list. Why? No one knew exactly. Two substitute names were needed. Gillespie chose.

Did fate intervene for Washington and Polling? Was this some great plan at work? Or was this just randomness pretending to be rationale?

According to Gillespie, he saw that Washington came from Newark, his own town. He didn't know the minister, but here was a chance to help a neighbor. It was as simple as that. Clark Polling was the son of a famous evangelist. Good PR to select this guy. Make the old man proud, too. That was all there was to it. Two names picked from a hat. The names were sent to Fort Miles Standish HQ. The machinery of life and death spun into action.

Strangely, the mission involving the *Dorchester* was so secret that not even the Colonel knew where the ship was going. He had a good idea but that's all. Gillespie didn't know something else. Against all possible odds, the "Four Chaplains" were about to be reunited at Camp Miles Standish before boarding the *Dorchester*.

All of them had attended the special Chaplain's school at Harvard University. Indeed, they had lived with each other in a dormitory called Perkins Hall. Before long, they ate together, studied together, and prayed together when they weren't drilling together. They bonded.

This unique situation, utterly new to the four men, It was best summed up by Rabbi Goode, who wrote to his wife as follows:

The arrangement proved to be a great source of liberal Education and it started on the very first morning. As each one of us began to recite his morning devotion, I suggested that, instead of each of us eyeing the other with curiosity, we should, rather, explain to each other what we were doing. This suggestion was readily accepted by all in the room, and our dormitory room became a classroom.

Now the men were together again about to sail on the *Dorchester.* What were the odds that four men from different parts of the country would room together at Harvard, then, after being dispatched to different bases as chaplains, would find themselves together again? What bookie would take such a bet?

For the Four Chaplains, though, all this was not a matter of fate working on some random basis. It was not simply a matter of coincidence, a statistical anomaly, which brought them together. Chance alone was not involved here. No, for them something more was at work. For the chaplains, it could only be a living God, who had placed them exactly where they would be most needed for the great challenge ahead. It was this faith in a loving God, which motivated and animated them. It was this faith, which ultimately gave them the courage to give their own lifejackets to others, to hold hands and praise God in those last moments before the *Dorchester* sank into the cruel North Atlantic.

It was this faith, which they shared with their congregations, their children, and most of all, their wives, the women who were at the core of their being and the love of their lives.

ISADORE FOX - COMMENTARY

It is difficult for me to talk about George. What to say? Where to start?

Let's begin on January 15, 1943, the day we were to celebrate our 19th anniversary of marriage. He was, I assumed, at Camp Miles Standish, where he was listed to go overseas, leaving me wondering if he had already sailed. It was difficult to know things in those days. Military secrecy and all that... To tell the truth, I had been praying, hoping he would not have to go.

I was working at a defense plant on our anniversary, when I received a bouquet of 19 roses. I looked all around for George, but couldn't see him. He was hiding, I learned later, behind a rather large man. He leaped out and surprised me. He had made it home for our wedding anniversary.

That night, cold chills ran up and down my spine as I lay beside him in bed, those last three nights he was with us. I just knew something was going to happen. I couldn't get the thought out of my mind. It kept stabbing at my heart.

George had to return to Camp Miles Standish. Before he left, he told me, "You do not need to take the long walk to the bus station on this cold morning. I would rather leave you here in the home that I am coming back to."

Knowing I couldn't argue with him, I just kissed him. I saw him walk a short way across the street into a heavy fog and disappear. That was the last time I saw my husband.

We were living in Gilman, Vermont, where George was a minister trying to get by on a extremely small salary, when the Japanese attacked Pearl Harbor. His response to the bombing was immediate, "Now we will go after them." From that terrible moment on, he applied for a commission in the Chaplains Corps of the United States.

I knew George had to serve God. That was his mission in life. I just kept asking myself if it was necessary for him to serve God on a battlefield?" At that time my husband was forty-one years old, a pretty old guy by military standards, and he had never really recovered from wounds received in the First World War. I knew, and George knew that the casualty rate among chaplains was extremely high. They didn't even carry a weapon. But God, I understood, had not placed them in the anguish of war to kill others. By his mercy, they were there to minister to the wounded and suffering, to tend to the hardships of men struggling to stay alive in a world of death.

I knew all this and I knew George had to enlist. He had once told me, "How little people seemed to understand that I am trying to live in the will of God, whatever the cost."

The cost proved to be very high.

On February 13, 1943, I was at home with my niece recording funny stories that would be sent to George. I hoped the stories would cheer him up. The stories never reached him. There was a knock at the door. I answered it. I was handed the dreadful telegram, beginning, "We regret to inform you...? George was missing in action. I collapsed on the bed. My world seemed to end in that one tragic moment. How could George be missing?

It was difficult for me to believe, since I had just received a letter from him, written, of course, earlier in the month. Apparently, the letter had been delayed in reaching me.

I am feeling fine in case you are wondering. I know you were anxious to hear from me. I haven't a trace of a cold any longer and I am seldom bothered with anything else... Many men come for counseling. This is the reason I am here and I am glad.

I could not believe George was dead. I wrote to the War Department, pleading with officials to see if my husband was alive.

I beg you in the name of my husband... and in name of our Eternal God and Heavenly Father to see to it that the War Department makes a further search for my husband to ascertain if he may not possibly be a German prisoner, or on some island in confinement where he cannot write or get a word to me.

In time, I came to accept my husband's death. At first, I did not want to live without George. I loved my children dearly. But with George gone there seemed to be a gap of a million miles between the children and me. He was nearly my whole life. I felt like a shadow without him.

People were calling him a hero. But I didn't want a hero. I wanted George. I already knew he was a hero, "the way he worked in those small churches and never complained, even when the pay was so small he could not get proper food and clothes for his children."

In time I decided to continue George's work in my own way. I attended the Boston University School of Theology and in 1955, I became an ordained minister. I was appointed to several parishes in New Hampshire and Vermont and also served as Chaplain of the American Legion Auxiliary in Vermont.

I never felt that I was carrying on George's work. But I did feel I as doing good and that he would be pleased and proud.

I still miss my husband. I still expect him to jump out from behind some larger man and surprise me with a bouquet of roses.

MARY WASHINGTON - COMMENTARY

Samuels submitted his first story to the *Chronicle* about Isadore Fox. It was an immediate sensation, especially with *Gold Star* mothers, and all women who had lost a loved one in the war, whether a sister, girlfriend, grandmother, or aunt. Even stout men found themselves entranced by the story of George Fox, his strength of conviction, his complete faith in God, and his willingness to sacrifice for others. Samuels had touched all of them, and no one more than his wife.

"Robert, you did an outstanding job. I'm so proud of you."

"I hope I can do as well with the next installment."

"You will."

It's difficult for me to discuss my son, John, Mary Washington had told Samuels by way of a letter. He often called me "his favorite girl." He took me to the movies on that fateful day, Sunday, December 7, 1941. We were driving home from a restaurant after the show, when he turned on the car radio. I think you know this. The news announcer said that America was at war. The Japanese had bombed our fleet in the Pacific. As I listened, I knew my three sons would surely enlist. John told me immediately, "Sorry, I've got to run. I've got to enlist."

I was so proud of John. He was an associate pastor to Father Murphy at St. Stephen's Church in Kearny, New Jersey. I knew Father Murphy, who had served in the Army during World War I, would support John's decision. It was support I dreaded.

Mothers, you know, are caught in the middle. Our first thought is to protect our children regardless of their age. At the same time we know we must let them make their own decisions. But it's not easy. If I had my own way no boy would go to war. I think mothers everywhere would agree. We give birth to our children. We raise them. Then to see them leave for war... It's too much.

Did you know John cheated to get into the Army? You did? Another source. Well, let me give you my perspective. John was always trying to prove he was a tough guy. That he could do anything the older boys did... He loved to pretend he was a big game hunter in Africa. He admired Frank Buck. As a boy, he was struck with a BB when playing the great African hunter. A stupid accident that left him with permanent damage to his right eye... From that time on he needed glasses. He hated them. The other boys made fun of him. That led to a few fights I can tell you and some salty Irish talk from me.

When he enlisted he was afraid his bad eye would keep him out of the Army when they gave him an eye test. You know what happened next. Another priest offered a solution, which John followed. He covered his bad eye twice and read the testing chart twice with his good eye. No one noticed anything. The deception worked. He would serve God, even if a little chicanery was needed to do it. But you know what I think. I bet they were on to John. I think they passed him on purpose. After all, he was going to be a Chaplain. Proper eyesight had little to do with that job. A good heart did.

He was impatient to go overseas. He was balking at the bit. He was always a little impetuous. He wrote to the Chaplains' office in Washington, requesting again the opportunity to serve outside of the country. I still remember the words: "Once more may I ask you to consider my application for overseas duty. If I am too fresh in requesting it, then slap me down." He wasn't slapped down. Instead, his request was honored. He went off to Camp Miles Standish.

In early February, I received a telephone message that John was missing in action. I remember screaming, "John's gone. John's gone." The pain was so great. Then, a few months later, I received another call. This time I was informed my second son, Francis, had been killed in the Pacific. A short time later, my third son, Leo, was missing in France. Eventually, he was found in a British hospital, He returned home, only to die shortly thereafter from his grievous wounds.

A friend told me about a Mrs. Bixby, who President Lincoln had written to concerning the loss of her five sons during the American civil war. I can only imagine what grief she experienced.

Of course, I knew about the five Sullivan "boys," who died on the *USS Alaska*. Those tragedies shared the pain, but did not eliminate it. Sometimes war asks too much of a mother.

I'm left with what the good priest, Father Bowden, later told me. He had talked about the dangers of the trip ahead with John before the *Dorchester* sailed. He pointed out the great blessing it would be to the soldiers, if anything happened, to have a priest on board to give them absolution. I hope that was true.

George is with God now. In so many ways, he always walked in His light. George never strayed. What happened on the *Dorchester* proved that beyond any question.

CHAPTER 21

HARD EVIDENCE

MID AUGUST 1942 - ARLINGTON, VIRGINIA

Harry had his man.

For two weeks now, the "bug" he had installed in Mr. Henry Fairfield's Washington condo had worked perfectly, much like a little bird singing its way through the morning haze. Careful as Fairfield might be, the bugging picked up and recorded sufficient damaging information to send the Source to jail for an extremely long time.

Then suddenly and unexpectedly, the "bug" had gone dead.

Harry had also placed hearing devices in the homes of Baldy and Nails, who had been bailed out of San Francisco's hospitality and had returned to the friendlier confines of Tennessee. Stretch had not escaped the technical prowess of Harry. He was also bugged.

In short order he had enough on all three KKK men to give them considerable jail time compliments of the taxpayer.

Of course, since Harry's work was covert and illegal, his evidence would never hold up in court. He knew that and didn't care. A courtroom was never on Harry's agenda. Other things were on his mind.

The Source found the "bug" quite by accident. His reading lamp had gone on the frizz, and while trying to fix it, the hearing device was found.

The Source checked out the device. It wasn't FBI hardware, nor was it some-thing used by the CIA. Careful and patient research by the Source indicated it was of Israeli manufacture, a device used by their special forces in covert operations.

Two questions pestered the Source. Who would want to bug him? Why was he being bugged? To answer the first question suggested he was now under suspicion, but by whom? Hoover? Robert Kennedy? Those two names came to mind immediately and just as quickly were discarded. Kurtz? A very remote possibility, at best... Hall and Brady? Anti-establishment as they were, still they were not rogue agents. As to the "why," no answer came to mind. To his knowledge, he hadn't slipped up. Bailing out Baldy and Nails was done through a second party in order to protect his identity. His connections to the KKK were buried deeply.

Yet, if he was being bugged, someone was on to him. One possibility was left for consideration, someone outside of government. If so, the "bug" was illegal and all recordings, if made, would be thrown out of court. Someone was acting outside of the law. That was the best possibility. But who was it? Sooner or later, the Source reasoned, that "someone" would approach him for money possibly or revenge. Either way, he would be ready for that day.

At the suggestion of the Source, Baldy and Nails, as well as Stretch, wasted no time in checking their homes and places of business for bugs. Though cleverly hidden, bugs were found. Again, as suggested by the Source, they instituted new rules. From now on, calls would be made only from outside pay phones. A rudimentary code would be used. For example, Robert Samuels was now "Fox 1," while the Source was "Hound Dog 1." Until directed, they would, as advised, remain quiet. Though desired, especially by Baldy, no further action would be taken against the reporter he had banged heads with in Mountain Lake Park.

Robert Samuels was safe for a while.

"He wants to go where?" an agitated Attorney-General asked Kurtz.

"Germany."

"Where exactly?"

"Kiel and Cologne."

"Why?"

"Unfinished business was all Samuels would tell me."

"Related to the book?"

"Yes."

"What does he want?"

"Passports and transportation."

"Anything else?"

"Everything we have on the *U-223*."

"Well, I guess we owe him that," Kennedy responded in a clipped voice. He's done us a great service. I want to meet that Irishman someday."

"Samuels is requesting our *U-223* records," the aide said to Hoover.

"Why?"

"He wants to meet with the survivors of the submarine."

"What the hell for?"

"He wants to tie up some loose pieces."

"Does he?" the Director asked in a snide way. Okay, let him take his little trip to Europe. We've got assets on the continent. We'll shadow him there."

"Instructions beyond that, Sir?"

"He can't come back with a 'smoking gun,' which would support the White House's push for civil rights legislation. Understood?"

"I'll pass the word."

"Look, Samuels, Germany is another ball of wax," Hill declared. "Are you sure you want to do this?"

"Yes."

"It's difficult for us to protect you on the continent," Brady confessed.

"It will be a fast trip."

"The Director doesn't want us to follow you to Kiel and Cologne," Hill said with finality. "That means he'll use other assets, maybe even the CIA."

"What about the KKK?" Samuels asked.

"They can reach that far, too," Hill said unreassuringly.

"Yes?" the man known as Bruno asked.

"You know what I want?" the distant voice from the Justice Department questioned.

"Yes. We have people in Germany to follow him."

"Good. Keep me informed. Refer to me only as Hound Dog 1."

"As you say, Sir."

CHAPTER 22

THE OTHER WIVES

LATE AUGUST 1962 – SAN FRANCISCO

Robert Samuels' story about Mary Washington's loss of three sons tugged at every reader's heart. Her sacrifice was simply too much to comprehend. President Lincoln's famous "altar of freedom" was demanding too much blood.

The price of freedom, Samuels wrote in his prologue to *The Other Wives*, was always brutal. A world safe from the Nazi Regime, Italy's fascists, and Japan's empire in the Pacific was proving, he wrote, "ever more costly as the last months of 1942 beckoned. Everywhere, the Allied forces were gradually stopping the forward march and menace of totalitarian thugs, but at such a price in flesh and treasure. In the shifting sands of North Africa, the bombed suburbs of Moscow, and in the malaria-plagued jungles of Guadalcanal the timeless struggles of civilizations hung in the balance." At such time, Samuels claimed, men reach for their God.

BETTY POLING

Where to begin? My husband Clark Poling, told me his departure from Camp Miles Standish would be delayed and he asked me to stay with him through the Christmas season and New Years. He

164

especially wanted me to bring our son, Corky. I jumped at the chance. He found two rooms in Taunton, which we could rent, and we spent a wonderful two months together.

After we returned to the family home in Schenectady, I received his last letter before he embarked on the Dorchester.

Dearest: I can't write a 'noble brave letter.' I would be a little self-conscious writing that sort of letter to you. All I can say is that always I will love you and hold our happy memories in the most sacred part of my thoughts until that time when we shall be together again...

It hadn't been easy for Clark to leave us. We had a three-year, Clark Jr., who we called Corky. I was pregnant with another baby that we had already nicknamed Thumper, after the rabbit in Bambi. But he had to go. He couldn't defy his conscience. His father, Daniel Poling, asked him why he was in such a hurry to enlist. I'll never forget his answer.

It is," he said, the love of America, love of freedom, love of home, love of justice, that will win for us. Lincoln proved that for Americans, proved and demonstrated it, and I must do my part.

I don't think people think this way anymore. But Clark did.

When he told me on the QT that he was going to Greenland, I was so happy. That was a relatively safe place to be in wartime. I felt good knowing he was in little danger.

Clark's last letter to me was both encouraging and frightening. The ground shifted under my feet as I read his last letter to me.

There is a part of my mind that is quite satisfied with the turn of events that send me to the safe but lonely post that we have talked about. However, you know there is another part of me that is disappointed. Perhaps all of us are drawn to the heroic and hazardous. I have done all and more than is legitimate to get into the tick of it... Dearest, I love you, and wherever I go and for all time I am yours, and you are mine. Read to Corky for me and spank him, love him, keep him away from the river, and feed him the oil! You must let me know how things are with "Thumper" and send me a wire. God bless you, my darling wife.

On April 10, 1942, I received a telegram indicating Clark was missing in action. A few weeks later, I gave birth to our daughter, Susan.

"Robert, what's the matter?" Lynn had asked her husband as he turned from the typewriter.

"Read this," he said.

Lynn took the typewritten page and read Clark Poling's last letter to his wife. In short order, she was brushing back tears.

"It's so beautiful," she said.

"And so painful," he admitted.

Through her tears, Lynn looked more closely at her husband. She knew the "quest" had taken a great deal out of him, but somehow, even more than she realized. He looked older and sadder, almost as if his soul was bearing the *Dorchester's* tragedy. She noticed more gray specks in his hair, and darker circles under his eyes. The lines in his forehead had deepened. Though he was eating well, he appeared thinner. Even his voice seemed toned down as if his breathing was laboring to enunciate the words. Lynn walked over to her husband and embraced him. They stayed that way, locked in each other's arms for the longest time. They clung to each other as Betty Poling and Clark had tried. They did not want to let go. They never wanted to let go. Life was too precious.

THERESA GOODE

Robert Samuels submitted the last article to the *Chronicle* in the waning days of August. He felt the series had been a success. Those who read about the four wives came to understand their Chaplain husbands, even as he had.

I want to tell you about my husband, Rabbi Alexander Goode. I'll start when we heard about Pearl Harbor. I nearly fell apart. Alex, the great patriot that he was, wanted to enlist immediately. That's when the road to Camp Miles Standish began. For my husband, there would be no turning back. He enlisted and eventually discovered his Greenland destination. How he learned this I don't know. But he was not happy about that, stating, "I don't want to go to a big cake of ice. I want to go where there's action."

I remember the day he left. It was a very difficult good-bye. I looked at him through the window of the train. I was crying and he was crying. I knew then I would never see him again. I just knew it in my heart.

Before he left the Camp, Alex sent me a final letter. In it he explained he was in a hurry. The men had just received notice to prepare for embarkation. He tried to allay my fears.

Don't worry. I'll be coming back much sooner than you think. Take care of yourself and the baby --- a kiss for each of you. I'll keep thinking of you. Remember, I love you very much.

Alex was always against bigotry and intolerance. He wanted to take steps to enlighten the uninformed. That was the message he gave his congregation. He felt the best cure against religious hatred was information. He said, "Let us know one another better and thus learn to appreciate the good inherent in every man."

He tried to put his beliefs into action. When our local Jewish community formed a Boy Scout troop, he refused to join in until it agreed to accept youths of all religions and races.

He believed in cultural pluralism long before it became a cultural buzzword. He believed that every group had made important contributions to America. He believed in democracy and felt it should have real meaning, where everyone would be everyone else's brotherly neighbor.

He was so idealistic. He so wanted a better world. He wanted a world where God touched each person through love and understanding.

He was a very special man and I miss him so terribly much.

CHAPTER 23

THE U-223

EARLY SEPTEMBER 1962 – GERMANY

"Ah Herr Samuels, a few weeks ago, about twenty-two days ago to be exact," Dr. Hoffman said with an air of complete confidence in his facts, "you made final preparations for a flight to Germany."

"I don't remember."

"You will. It was just after you were nominated for a Pulitzer Prize."

"Robert, this is so wonderful," Lynn exclaimed. "What an honor."

"Nice," Matt said in his own cool way.

"I knew you would be considered," Rachel said, "the series on the wives was just too good."

"Well, let's see what happens," Samuels replied. "Either way, you guys are a great fan club."

"The best," Lynn said with a big smile. "Kieran, what do you think?"

Kieran gave Samuels a 'thumbs-up.' The gesture said it all.

"How ironic, isn't it, Herr Samuels, "that you would be nominated for a 'prize' established by a Hungarian-American with, I assure you, German blood flowing through his veins. After all, it was a German torpedo which sank the *Dorchester* and led to your series on the chaplain's wives in the first place."

"Chaplains…?"

"Four of them," interrupted Bruno with obvious delight. "All sent to the bottom of the Atlantic."

"I'm afraid he's right, Herr Samuels. Wartime is so cruel."

Try as he might, Samuels couldn't brush aside the fuzzy cobwebs of his mind. He pushed and pried his memory, but, except for teasing images, which fluttered momentarily before him, nothing solid emerged. For the moment, at least, his efforts were an exercise in futility.

Observing him, Dr. Hoffman, understood Samuels' frustration as he battled the fall-induced short-term amnesia. In time the patient's doctor knew Samuels would remember. Samuels just needed more prodding.

"Herr Samuels, you booked a Pan American flight to London's Heathrow Airport, a few days later. A first class ticket was arranged for you.

The flight to Europe had aspects of a "milk run" for Samuels. The big Boeing 727 flew directly to St. Louis for a two-hour layover before heading for New York, where Samuels stayed overnight. The next day the jet cruised across the Atlantic at 30,000 feet before touching down on British soil. Again, after resting for the night, Samuels hopped on a local flight to Kiel, Germany.

As he flew across the English Channel, he thought about what had brought him to the continent. He had come to see a survivor of the war and the *U–223*, one Kurt Roser, who had, at the command of the captain, ordered three torpedoes launched against the *Dorchester*. The *U–223* was 1,000 yards away from the troopship when the order was given. Unfortunately for the convoy, only two torpedoes went wide. Such were the grim statistics of war.

The *U–223*'s keel was laid down in July 1941 in Kiel, where the F. Krupp Company built it. It was commissioned almost a year later,

June 6, 1942, exactly two years before the D – Day and the Allied invasion of "fortress Europe." Two captains would command the submarine before the war ended.

The first captain, Karl-Jurg Wachter, would be highly decorated with the Iron Çross and the German Cross of Gold for successfully sinking four ships over the course of an equal number of patrols. In total, Wachter spent 155 days at sea. The ships destroyed besides the *Dorchester* were the *Winkler, Stanmore*, the *HMS Cuckmore* (K 299). The tonnage lost amounted to18, 826 tons.

Wachter was a young, inexperienced officer, who wanted naval fame by sinking as many Allied ships as possible. He hoped to please Grand Admiral Karl Donitz, who was the mastermind behind the "wolf pack" strategy so devastating to American and British shipping. Apparently, Wachter was on personal terms with the Donitz. Assigned to "torpedo alley," his charge was to stop Allied supplies and troops from reaching Greenland

The next and last commander was Peter Gerlach, who took over the *U – 223* on January 12,1944. At the time, he was one of the youngest U-boat commanders during the war. He spent over 40 days at sea during two patrols. He wasn't a lucky skipper. No Allied ships were sunk.

However, on March 30, 1944, during a brutal naval battle with British warships, a salvo of torpedoes fired at the *HMS Leforey (G 99)* by the *U – 223* proved successful in sinking the destroyer with a terrible loss of life. Over 180 officers and seaman were killed.

The *U – 223* did not escape from this engagement. The day before, on March 29th, the *U – 223* was located by the *HMS Ulster's* radar some 60 nautical miles northeast of Palmero, Italy. Two other destroyers composed the *14th Flotilla*, the doomed *Leforey* and the *HMS Tumult*.

The *U – 223* was heavily depth-charged but, against all odds, it managed to carry out evasive maneuver in an attempt to evade further detection. On the following day, joined by still more British ships, the submarine was forced to surface and was attacked by the destroyers with gunfire. The *U – 223* was unable to stand the deadly barrage and was sunk.

In its waning movements of life, just before she found a last home beneath the seas, the submarine fired the fateful torpedoes at the *Leforey*. The *U–223* suffered 23 dead, but twenty-seven seamen survived. The captain, Peter Gerlach, went down with his ship. Two of the survivors were Kurt Roser and Gerhard Buske.

The *U – 223* was one of 784 German submarines lost during the war with the loss of over 28,000 officers and seamen. Of the survivors, over 5,000 became prisoners of war. The terrible losses suffered by the German navy were equally off set by the disastrous pain inflicted on the Allies. Over 30,000 Allied merchant marine sailors died and 2,603 merchants ships were sunk. Well over 13 ½ million tons was destroyed.

As Samuels reflected on the *U - 223*, and the savage naval struggle for control of the North Atlantic, one somber thought lingered in his mind. Unlike a land battle, which, following a deadly engagement leaves the ground pitted with shell holes and burned out equipment, and the bloody bodies of once vibrant young men, sea battles cast few reminders of what took place. On land there is a constant presence of the sacrifice and in time, if the dead are to be honored, a memorial cemetery is established. At sea, there is little to recall the frightful battles beyond floating debris and bloated bodies, which in time disappear into the depths.

Conflict at sea was a lonely war.

Samuels' thoughts were interrupted by the plane's P.A. system. "We will be landing in Kiel in ten minutes."

CHAPTER 24

ROSER

SEPTEMBER 1962 - KIEL, GERMANY

"Herr Samuels, you're starting to remember?" Dr. Hoffman asked in his usual comforting way.

"I ..."

"Yes, I can see you're glimpsing the past."

"It's about time," Bruno said in a huff. "Perhaps I can prod his recollections a little."

"Patience, Bruno. Herr Samuels is healing nicely. We don't want to unnecessarily interfere with his progress."

"As you say, doctor."

Samuels heard the exchange between the two men. On a medical level, it made sense to him. His memories were beginning to return, but not as a complete picture. Rather, more like a puzzle, one piece here, another piece there, and only occasionally two pieces fitting together. But on another level, their words had a malevolent tone to them. Suspicion grew in Samuels' mind, as did anxiety.

Dr. Hoffman interrupted Samuels' thoughts. "Let's talk about Kiel, Herr Samuels. You remember your visit to see Kurt Roser, don't you?"

The name had a familiar ring to it. Samuels had heard the name before and he recalled coming to Kiel, but why?

The airport in Kiel was on the outskirts of the city. As had been arranged with Roser, the former U-boat officer was waiting for him at the baggage claim carousel.

"Mr. Roser."

"Herr Samuels."

Samuels grabbed his suitcase and followed Roser into a dining area, where the two men found an unobtrusive corner table for the privacy their meeting demanded. When the waitress arrived, Roser smiled and said, "Permit me to order, Herr Samuels." He did so in a strong German accent.

"I ordered our best beer, much stronger than that stuff they make in Cologne. I took the liberty of asking for a meat dish, too. Our famous thick Kiel stew with large chunks of pork, laced with ripe carrots and splendid, baby potatoes, and garnished with an excellent sauce, which, I trust, will be to your liking."

"I can hardly wait. Your English, by the way, is excellent. I'm afraid my German is kaput."

"Not to worry, Herr Samuels. After the war, I continued my training in engineering and took English language courses. And, of course, I have been to America."

Samuels was stunned. This was news to him. Nothing in his file on Roser indicated time spend in the USA.

"You look surprised, Herr Samuels."

"I am."

"A simple explanation, really. I was one of a few survivors when the British sent the *U−223* to the bottom in 1944. I was dragged out of Atlantic, thrown into irons, repatriated to the Americans, and sent to your state of Mississippi, where I picked cotton and sandbagged the Mississippi River as a prisoner-of-war. I learned a little English during my enforced stay."

"Mississippi, I'll be."

"My best friend, Gerhard Buske, who lives in Cologne, also survived. He endured the last years of the war as a POW in Canada."

"Thankfully, you both survived."

"You will visit him after you leave Kiel?"

"Yes."

As they talked, their food arrived in a good size tankard for the beer, and a heavy ceramic bowl containing the stew. With a wink from Roser, he dove into the stew, which was even better than advertised as was the beer he washed it down with. Roser watched him with devour the meal.

"You were hungry, Herr Samuels?"

"Yes. I hope my table manners don't offend you."

"Not in the least."

As he ate, Samuels glanced at his German guest. In some respects they were, he thought, as they talked, look-a-likes --- about the same age and height, a little thinning of the hair, and both of a quiet, even serious nature.

"Did you enjoy the food in Mississippi?"

"A lot of fish, which was fine with me, since the citizens of Kiel straddle the Baltic Sea and seafood is a large part of our diet."

"And stew."

"Yes, and stew."

"How did you like America?"

"Herr Samuels," he said, "it was a wonderful place to be as a POW, much better than a Russia retreat in Siberia. But still, I was a prisoner and my country was at war, and your bombers were devastating our cities, including Kiel."

"You lost family?"

"Sadly, yes."

For a few moments the two men turned to their food, eating in silence, hearing only the music panned through the P.A. system. In time, Roser said, "May I tell you a story?"

"Of course."

"You know the city of Hattiesburg in Mississippi?"

"Yes."

"It happened at lunch. Along with other German POW's, we were having our noon meal in a local café compliments of your federal government. As we ate, a truckload of black soldiers arrived. I believe you refer to them as Negroes. Anyway, they were denied entrance because of their color, and were forced to get bag lunches in the back of the restaurant."

"We have our problems," Samuels said.

"I found it astounding and amusing, after all, the Nazi regime. as your country referred to Germany, was supposed to adhere to a racial philosophy. How ironic, then, was it for me to witness racism is America."

"We're still learning how to get along."

"As, Herr Samuels, are our countries."

The waitress arrived at that moment and refilled their tankards, and suggested a black forest cake for dessert, fashioned by their own baker, who was known in Kiel as a wizard with after meal delights. They happily accepted her suggestion.

"Mr. Roser, again thank you for meeting with me."

"How could I not meet with you? Your letter and the materials you sent me about the Four Chaplains was too much to pass up. Now, what is it you want to know?"

"First, I'd like to know about the immediate events leading up to the torpedoing of the *Dorchester.*"

"A terrible incident, Herr Samuels, one I will take to my grave. Though it had to be done, no naval officer takes joy in sinking a troopship.

We were on the surface and stalking the convoy at night when we could use of diesel engines and deploy the snorkel, which brought in fresh air. We were about 1,000 yards behind what your navy identified as convoy SG – 24.

Many people hold a misunderstanding about submariners, a romantic notion, if you will. The truth is far from it. Consider this, 50 or more men enclosed in a dark, cramped underwater steel tube, most of them with grease on their clothes and smeared on their faces. They live in constant fear that a surface ship will drop a load of depth charges on them which, when they explode, rip open your submarine as if it were a can of sardines. It was not by accident that submariners were nicknamed the "suicide service," since life expectancy was only fourteen months, and where 60 out of 100 men would die. I once came across a US Postal Stamp that commemorated this struggle between the sailors on the surface and the submariners below.

But back to the *Dorchester*... It was dark and misty, a deep haze which made it difficult for us to observe the convoy clearly. We were unsure of the convoy's destination. Our spies in Saint John's thought it might be occupied Norway or Denmark, but by the time the *Dorchester* got to "torpedo junction," we were very sure it was Greenland. The *Dorchester* was riding low in the water, which meant it was fully loaded. Since she was a coast steamer, we concluded she was carrying troops rather than petrol or coal. The Captain was unsure he wanted to waste a torpedo on it. He hoped to use his torpedoes on larger ships.

I was standing with Captain Wachter in the conning tower when he made his decision. He gave the command, "Flood the active torpedo tubes." At 12:55 a.m. the order was given to fire. We had a clear shot. No screening ship was in our way. And we hadn't been picked up on radar. A spread of three torpedoes was fired. Only one hit but that was enough. It hit below the waterline. A fatal explosion occurred almost immediately.

～

Roser paused to what he would say next. The man seemed exhausted. It was not easy for him to retell the tragic events of that night, February 3, 1943. Nor was it easy for Samuels to listen. Gathering himself, Roser continued.

～

We immediately plunged into the depths, leveling off at about 500 feet where we used our batteries and tried to evade the surface ships by running silent. Most of us believed the hunter had now become the hunted, and that we would soon die from a bursting depth charge. Somehow we survived the night, eight hours in a hot metal tube with stale air and fearful hearts.

We knew what was happening on the surface. A man can only

last for 20 minutes in the North Atlantic before he freezes to death. There was nothing we could do for those men. Had we surfaced to save them, the escort ships would have fired at us. Quite frankly, we never understood why the screening ships chased us rather than immediately rendering assistance to men in the water. So many more could have been saved.

~

Samuels had to ask the question. "How did you feel about sinking a troopship?"

Roser surprised him with his answer. "Let me ask you, how did you feel about 1,000 heavy bombers, your B - 17's, dropping death from the skies over German cities?"

"I ..."

"I'm sure, Herr Samuels, you felt justified because our nations were at war. The same was true for us. We were trying to starve England, and get the British to drop out of the war. Our submarines and Condor planes were trying to strangle the shipping lanes and to forestall the invasion of Europe. We wanted Germany to survive."

What could Samuels say? Nations justify in wartime what they would never permit in peacetime. Whatever the causes of war, once engaged it is a struggle to the end. It was difficult, Samuels reasoned, to claim the higher moral ground. War tends to muddy all sides.

"May I ask you, Mr. Roser, how you feel about the Four Chaplains?"

"From your reports, I can only believe they were extraordinary men, who were willing to sacrifice for others. Their story is special, one that should not be forgotten. But I must caution you. There were in our forces other men who sacrificed their lives for others. It is an uncommon valor, which, I think, is common to all armies at war. Somehow in the most tragic of events, the best of the human spirit arises. In that sense, all such men are immortal, don't you think?"

Samuels nodded in agreement.

The two men, sharing dark truths, drank the last of their beer and ate the remaining cake crumbs. There was little else they could do. The past could not be undone.

"By the way, Herr Samuels, did I tell you that Kiel is the capital of Schleswig-Holstein, the most populous and northern German state?"

"I don't think you mentioned it."

"We're 56 miles from Hamburg and attached to three bodies of water, the South shore of the Baltic Sea, the Jutland peninsula, and the Kiel fjord, which is the busiest artificial waterway in the world, or so our city fathers say. And the city is a little older than your country. The city of Kiel was founded in 1233. Count Adolf IV, if my memory is correct, provided the aristocratic push to make it happen. His son, John I granted the city its charter in 1242. Just a little city trivia."

"As I recall, Kiel was controlled by Denmark until 1864, when a confederation of Austria and Prussia snatched it away. During the Austro-Prussian War of 1866, Prussia proved stronger and took over the area. It became part of modern Germany after Prussia defeated France in 1870."

"Very good, Herr Samuels. You know our history."

Samuels shrugged and said, "Some." He then asked a question which had been on his mind throughout the meeting.

"Mr. Roser, if the opportunity arose to meet the relatives of the Four Chaplains, and possibly survivors of the *Dorchester*, would you be interested in some form of reconciliation?"

"Would they be interested in meeting me, Herr Samuels? Perhaps that is the more difficult question. We mustn't forget, I participated in the death of their loved ones."

"But if it could be arranged?"

"With trepidation, yes."

"Good."

"And the purpose for this meeting, Herr Samuels?"

"Forgiveness and redemption."

Roser let Samuels' words settle before responding.

"You Americans have term, 'two-way street," I believe."

"We do."

"Will the *Dorchester* survivors, and the families be willing to walk on such a street?"

"I hope so."

"That is all I can ask. Now, I have a favor to ask of you, Herr Samuels."

"If I can."

When you are in Cologne meeting with my old friend, Gerhard Buske, our first officer on *the U – 223*, please ask him about the photographs he's promised to send me."

"Photographs?"

"Gerhard was a professional photographer before the war. He was a very good one. Whenever the Captain would permit him, he would take pictures of the crew and even some during action."

"Did he take pictures the night the *Dorchester* was sunk?"

"Possibly. You must ask him."

"But they couldn't have survived, could they? The *U–223* was sunk."

"Knowing Gerhard, anything was possible."

CHAPTER 25

PACIFIST

SEPTEMBER 1962 – COLOGNE, GERMANY

"Bruno, look, Herr Samuels is remembering."

"Finally, doctor."

Indeed, Samuels' memory was flooding back now, a torrent of images, sounds, and ideas in a kind of cognitive free-for-all within his brain. At a faster rate now, the puzzle pieces were locking into place, reminding Samuels where he had been and why.

"Get him to tell us about the photograph," Bruno railed. "We must know what he did with it."

"As always, Bruno, you are in a hurry," Dr. Huffman said. "We have time. Herr Samuels isn't going anywhere. Anyway, we need to know more about Gerhard Buske, and the movement he leads."

Samuels took a high-speed train from Kiel to Cologne in a generally southern route following the Rhine River, Germany's great waterway and, at times, a historic defensive moat against invaders from the west. As his train rocketed down the tracks, Samuels considered what little he knew about Cologne.

It was the fourth largest city after Berlin, Hamburg, and Munich, but it is the largest city in the German Federal State of North

Rhine-Westphalia. Certainly, it was one of Europe's oldest cities having been founded in 38 B.C. The city's famous Cathedral was the seat of the Archbishop of Cologne. The University of Cologne was one of Europe's oldest and most renown.

Not much, Samuels thought, not much at all.

Gerhard Buske, as planned, was waiting for Samuels at the Cologne Central Railroad Station situated near the revitalized older section of the city, which had been hit particularly hard during the Allied bombing raids. Buske was waiting for Samuels inside the station. He recognized Samuels from a newspaper picture he was holding. Samuels joined his German host in one of the station's newer restaurants. After ordering beers, plus cheese and crackers, Buske got right down to business.

"You know, Herr Samuels, pay no attention to whatever Kurt told you about Kiel's beer and food. Nothing can compare to what we make in Cologne."

"Perhaps I should take a neutral position."

"A prudent and safe decision," I think. "Now lets talk about other things, yes?"

"Yes."

As Buske spoke, it was hard for Samuels to see him as some terrible ogre in an underwater cylinder of death, who had actually pushed the buttons to destroy the *Dorchester*. He look more like an accountant or engineer, mild-mannered and studious, not a goose-stepping Hun devouring a continent in the name of "national socialism" as preached by the Nazi regime.

"Herr Samuels, I read your reports on the *Dorchester*, and certainly the actions taken by the Four Chaplains, as well as what you wrote about the wives of those men. I must say I was impressed with your research and, if I might point out, the delicate hand you showed in portraying the chaplains."

"I appreciate your thoughts."

"Kurt and I also appreciated the way you've handled the *U-223*. You did not demonize the ship and its crew. You did not describe them as evil incarnate. For that I thank you."

"As were the Coast Guard cutters depth charging the *U-223*, everyone was just doing his job."

"Young men below the surface and above put into impossible situations by the failure of their governments to resolve issues peacefully."

"I couldn't agree more, Herr Buske."

"Now, as you Americans like to say, lets cut to the chase. You want to know about the *U – 223?*"

"Not exactly."

"What, then?"

"After the war, when you learned about the troopship and the terrible loss of life, how did that affect you? Please start at this point."

Buske steadied himself before speaking. "At the risk of appearing schizophrenic, a man with multiple personalities, I will answer your question from two perspectives, which unfortunately are in conflict with each other. The sinking of the *Dorchester* did not weigh on my mind. I was a professional sailor, an officer in Germany's navy. We were at war.

"My family was living in Cologne, a major German military area and an Allied bombing target during the war. Cologne endured 262 air raids, which caused more than 20,000 civilian casualties, including members of my family. The entire center of the city was destroyed.

"The worst raid occurred during the night of May 31, 1942, when the city was the site of "Operation Millennium," the first thousand-plane attack on a city by the Royal Air Force. The bombers came at night. They attacked Cologne with 1,455 ton of high explosives. The raid lasted for 75 minutes and made over 60,000 people homeless. Over 500 people were killed.

"This painful memory was on my mind when I released the torpedoes, which sank the *Dorchester*. Not revenge, exactly. And, bear with me, not merely getting even. That would never be possible. I was just doing my job as I had been trained to do, much like the British pilots who flew over my city. So that is one perspective."

"After the war, I returned to what was left of Cologne and slowly, as the horrors of the death camps became known at the Nuremburg Trials, I had what theologians call an epiphany. I determined to never serve the god of war again. My life, to the extent I could, would serve justice and peace. I became a pacifist and have remained so to this day.

"I was especially affected by your research into the *Dorchester* tragedy. I read about your Coast Guard Cutters finding frozen men, who from all appearances seemed to be alive and drifting with the waves, lit up like Christmas trees with their blinking red lights, as if they were enjoying the festivities celebrating Christ's life. But they were not alive. The sea was a vast graveyard of joyful lights and dead bodies."

Samuels was profoundly affected by Gerhard's confession. The man was obviously torn between past duties as a naval officer and his present obligations as a citizen of the world. In pacifism, he had found a path between the two fires.

"You have more than answered my question, Mr. Gerhard."

"Then let me ask you a question, Herr Samuels.

"Of course."

"Do you believe in good and evil?"

"Not in an absolute sense, but only as I can view events and the behavior of others."

"Dropping bombs on Cologne?"

"A justified evil."

"Sinking the *Dorchester?* Another justified evil?"

"Unfortunately."

"So Herr Samuels, there is no universal evil? Or good?"

"It is difficult to have moral certainty."

"All is relative?"

"Absoluteness is difficult achieve. There is what we choose to call evil. The 'final solution' was evil. No justification supports death camps."

"And Herr Samuels, the internment of Japanese-Americans in your country?"

"An evil, a lesser evil, and inadequately justified."

"Supported by the American people?"

"Most at first after the shock of Pearl Harbor. Less in time."

"Dropping an atomic bomb? Killing defenseless civilians, Herr Samuels?"

"To save many thousands more if Japan had been invaded, yes, a case can be made for using the bomb."

"Do you make such a case."

"After Okinawa, I just wanted to go home. I didn't think I'd survive the invasion of Japan, planned for 1946."

"The two atomic bombs saved you?"

"Most probably, yes."

"And our V-2 rockets which crashed into London, indiscriminately killing and injuring thousands of civilians, We hoped they would end the war, too. We justified their use, too."

Now the two men merely looked at each other. They had reached an impasse. Complete moral clarity eluded them. They agreed that both good and evil existed and that no universal moral law existed in absolute terms, since behavior was a matter of individual choice and always relative to what others were doing. This was especially true in wartime. Their unfulfilling conclusion left them saddened.

"We seem to have an ethical dilemma," Herr Samuels.

"True enough, but a moral person must make distinctions and in so doing, weigh the consequences of his actions. I can think of only one human emotion, which might resolve the situation."

"And what is that?"

"Empathy. To a degree, we have the capacity to understand the plight of others and, at the very least, to avoid inflicting pain on our fellow humans."

"By what standard do you do this, Herr Samuels?"

"We take a stand for life."

"To what end?"

"Redemption. We make peace, if possible, with what we have done, and with an imperfect world."

"Is that why you are writing a book about the Four Chaplains, Herr Samuels?

"At the beginning, no. Now, very much so."

"Perhaps it is why I lead a pacifist movement."

"Perhaps, Herr Buske."

Almost as an after thought, Samuels said, "Mr. Roser would very much like you to send him the photos you promised."

"I have been lax."

"If I may ask, how did you save the photos?"

"Another story, Herr Samuels. As you already know, the *U-223* was picked up on British radar units on January 29, 1944. For two days we were harassed by depth charges and the constant pinging of their radar. No matter how deep we dived, the destroyers continued to circle above us. With our batteries running low, we had to finally surface the next day. The British were waiting for us."

"I was a professional photographer before the war. The *U-223's* two captains, Wachter and Gerlach, permitted me to pursue my wartime avocation whenever possible. To safeguard my negatives in case of an emergency, I built a water-tight box, which I grabbed before we surfaced. The box was returned to me after the war once I was no longer a POW in Canada. The pictures were unharmed in their sanctuary. How they were saved in the first place I do not know."

"Did you take a photo of the *Dorchester*?" Samuels asked.

"Only one and through the periscope about fifteen minutes after our attack. Perhaps earlier."

"You still have that picture?"

"Of course."

"May I..."

Buske removed a business-size envelope from his sport coat and handed it to Samuels. "This is for you, Herr Samuels. Another step toward settling the past, I hope. Kurt told me you might ask for the photograph."

Samuels held his breath as he opened the envelope and took out a photograph. Taken in the night and against the backdrop of partial moonlight, the photo showed the *Dorchester* already beginning to tilt toward her eventual death plunge. Try as he might, Samuels could discern little beyond a cluster of five men, who appeared to be holding hands on the top deck. The photo provided no clarity as to who the men were. Further amplification and refinement would probably prove insufficient in making a determination.

Five men, Samuels thought, approximately fifteen minutes after the attack. The timing was right. Could this be the smoking gun he was searching for? If so, again the evidence was circumstantial. Historical truth, as always, was proving to be an elusive commodity. Still, it was something tangible, a physical reminder of that terrible, unholy night, which brought out the best in five brave men. It would have to suffice.

"The photo helps, Herr Samuels?"

"I think so."

"Then perhaps, redemption awaits both of us."

CHAPTER 26

MISSING

SEPTEMBER 1962 – USA

"He's what?" the Director asked his aide incredulously.

"He's disappeared, Sir."

"Elaborate."

"He was meeting with two survivors of the *U – 223*."

"Roser and Buske?"

"Correct."

"And?"

"He vanished into thin air after seeing Buske."

"Where?"

"Cologne."

"What about the CIA? I thought they were watching his back."

"They were."

"So?"

"They lost him, Sir."

"Contact Hill and Brady."

"I don't believe it," Kurtz said, almost spitting out the words. "How could this happen?"

"We don't know," responded Hill."

"The Director didn't explain Brady said, anger rising in his voice. "He wanted you to know he's contacting our assets in Germany."

"Jesus Christ, what am I going to tell his family?" Kurtz lamented.

"Don't say anything," Hill volunteered. "At least not until we know what's going on."

"Keep them in the dark?" Kurtz asked.

"Exactly," Brady said.

"One day only," Kurtz said. "Now I have the joy of sharing our good news with the Attorney-General."

"Find him," Robert Kennedy said in a voice strong enough to chill the dead. "You're the head of the CIA. Talk to Kurtz. Contact Hoover. Do whatever it takes, but find him. I don't want Samuels washing up in the Rhine."

"The Agency will find him."

"It better, or that ugly stuff is going to hit the fan."

"That's right," the Source said triumphantly. "He's missing, Stretch."

"Our German contacts came through."

"Without question."

"The photo?"

"They're still looking for it."

"And Samuels?"

"He may have an accident," the Source said.

"I understand, Brady. He's MIA."

"Harry, can you get to the Source?"

"Yes."

"Do it."

"Consider it done,"

"I bet Dad is having a great time in Germany," Rachel said. He always wanted to visit Europe."

"I hear the women are great looking," Matt said smiling. "Maybe I can go to Germany some day."

"Knowing your dad, he's probably in a library with his head buried in books, " Lynn said smiling. "Or at least that's where he better be."

"That's right doctor," the Source muttered, "the CIA is involved."

"And INTERPOL?"

"Probably."

"No matter, we're almost done."

"The photograph?"

"Close."

"Good."

"You heard me, Kurt," Gerhard said. "The police just left. Herr Samuels is missing."

"They left me five minutes ago."

"They're moving quickly. They'll find him."

"Gerhard, did you give him the photograph?"

"Yes, as we planned."

"He believes it's the $U-223$?"

"Of course, Kurt."
"Good."

"We need to talk."
"Who are you?"
"Just call me Harry."
"Who?"
"Not your friend."
"What?"
"Three hours ago, you were with Kurtz."
"How..."
"Later you made a call to Tennessee."
"I ..."
"Where is Robert Samuels?"
"There is no need for that gun," the Source said fearfully.
"On the contrary, there is every need."
"Please..."
"I repeat, where is Samuels?"

"That's it, then," Brady said to the Director.
"A private hospital near his hotel?"
"Yes."
"You just learned about this?"
"My contact called me five minutes ago."
"Credible?"
"Very. Make the call."

Ten minutes later, the Director of the FBI spoke to his counterpart, the director of INTERPOL

CHAPTER 27

SURVIVAL

SEPTEMBER 1962 – COLOGNE, GERMANY

"Herr Samuels, you have remembered."

Dr. Hoffman said it as a fact, not a question. He was not wrong. Seemingly in a blink of an eye, Samuels recalled everything.

"No need to pretend otherwise."

"You're right. The time for pretense is over."

"Excellent. You will tell me what I want to know. Where is the photo Buske gave to you?"

"Let me take my knuckles to him," Bruno said sharply.

"You've already tried that," Samuels replied, almost casually.

Following his talk with Buske, Samuels had gone to his hotel, the Cologne Ritz, which catered to American tourists and businessmen. After speaking with the concierge, he went to his room to unpack and rest before getting at his notes. Without warning, the door burst open and two men entered. One had a gun, which he trained on Samuels. The other, who Samuels now knew as Bruno, held a sap, dark and mean looking.

"Where's the photo, Samuels?"

"What photo?"

It had been a dumb response. Cat-like in his movements for a big man, Bruno came at Samuels and wacked him across the forehead knocking him head first into a solid, metal heater and out cold. What was intended by Bruno to be unadulterated physical intimidation turned in an instant to utter frustration and unexpectedconfusion. Instead of reviving quickly, Samuels slumped into something akin to a coma. He was in no condition to respond to their questions or their threats. Two bumps on the head had seen to that. Unable to pry anything from Samuels, the two men were forced to quietly remove him from the hotel later that night. They carried him out, two old friends taking care of a buddy who had too much to drink. The ruse worked. No one was the wiser.

"Now I know how I got here, Herr Doctor," Samuels said sarcastically, "but I don't know where I am exactly."

"You're in a private hospital in the suburbs of Cologne," Hoffman said in a voice no longer friendly. "A very private hospital. Indeed, you are the only patient at this time."

"Just you and us," Bruno said as he flexed his shoulder muscles. "No one to hear you yell."

Samuels realized what was happening. Again, they were using intimidation to frighten him and make him talk. And it was working. He was scared out of his mind by these creeps. For no good reason, he decided to stall for time. As a kid, he had seen numerous westerns where, thundering out of Hollywood's version of the "Old West," the blue-clad cavalry arrived, swords drawn and rifles spurting bullets at the last split second to rescue the endangered wagon train and a damsel in distress. In the recesses of Samuels' mind, he hoped life's script had John Wayne galloping toward him, even if the "Wild West" was now east of the Rhine River.

"Who are you jokers?" Samuels asked caustically. "From what I can, you're just a couple of what we Americans call punks. You know, crap."

"Crap," stormed Huffman, "I am a physician."

"Who hangs around with a junior King Kong, and holds a person against his will. Some professional, you are, Sir. You're nothing more than a hired hand with rather poor bedside manners. In short, you're a fraud."

"Let me at him, Herr Doctor."

"No, Bruno, I need to find out who he is working with."

"But, we waste time."

"It will be time well wasted."

Doctor Hoffman's ego had been tarnished, just as Samuels hoped. The good doctor could not let such a jab go unanswered.

"I am a graduate of one Berlin' finest medical schools, but that is besides the point. More importantly, I am the acknowledged leader of the "Germany First" movement in Cologne, an organization determined and destined to revive the greatness of the Third Reich."

"You're a Nazi throwback," Samuels said laughingly. "If you haven't heard, Herr Adolf died in a bunker."

"You American fool. A man died, not his ideas."

"National Socialism, give me a break."

"You mock me."

"History mocks you, Herr Doctor. Fascism is a discarded relic of the past, a mere footnote today to an inglorious decade, not your boss' 'thousand year reign.'"

Samuels knew he was on slippery ground. He needed to keep Hoffman talking, while hoping his trained ape wouldn't sap him again. Samuels understood he was walking a tight rope. Oh, God, he thought, where are the Marines?

"Herr Samuels, not only is fascism alive in Germany, it is also at home in your country."

"No chance."

"How do you think we found you? How did we know what you were doing in Germany? It was no accident that we followed you in Kiel and Cologne. We know all about your meetings with Roser and Buske."

"Luck!" Samuels said, knowing it was more than that.

"No, a high source in your own government, a prominent official, who just happens to share our racial views and disgust for degenerate societies composed of the impure mixing of inferior racial groups with a superior majority. We want to get rid of North Africans and Moslems from Turkey, not to mention drug users and homosexuals. We want to cleanse our society. We want national regeneration. We want, it seems, what your own KKK desires, a nation dominated by Arians; that is, the white majority."

"You're off your rocker."

"Am I? Our source is a member of the KKK. He believes in a strong nationalistic, authoritarian view of government, where an elite can provide the strong leadership needed to survive in a Darwinian world of perpetual racial and economic conflict. He is a Nazi in spirit and deed."

"Okay, but what does that have to do with me. I'm a reporter researching a book about Four Chaplains who died long ago. What in God's name does that have to do with your fascist fantasies?"

"Foolish man, do you really think we want, that the KKK wants a civil rights bills passed in your country? Do you think we want a black face on a new stamp? Do you think we want social harmony? The brotherhood of man is not what we are after. What we want is racial tensions. We want social violence. We want chaos and confusion in your cities. We want your white majority to rise up in righteous glory and rid itself of those Africans. That's why you cannot be permitted to carry home a photo to support your claims about the *Dorchester's* cook."

"Doctor, you speak too much," Bruno said finally. "He stalls. We need to know about the photo."

"You quite right, Bruno. Let's take him to the roof."

Christ, thought Samuels, these guys make the "far right" at home look like flaming liberals. The business about an official with KKK ties was, however, disturbing. Someone, as he thought, had been on his backside since the whole business began. The attempted beating in the park was no accident. Bruno's sap was not a mirage. There was, he could not deny, a connection. There was a mole in our government. No, a spy, a damn traitor, who had sold him out and put his life in jeopardy. What had Hoffman said? "Take him to the roof." What, dear God, was on the roof?

Samuels had to think quickly. Earlier a seed had been planted in his unconsciousness, which he had dismissed as silly, as improbable, but perhaps a way to save himself. Now, as the idea percolated into the rational part of his mind, it seemed the only possible thing to do.

Summing all his strength, Samuels kicked out against the surprised doctor forcing his wheelchair to surge backward toward a small metal bureau, which he hoped contained medical supplies. Thank God for Newton's "second laws of physics." The startled doctor crumbled from the unexpected blow to his shins, while Samuels flew backwards before colliding with a metal bureau. Even as Bruno advanced on him, Samuels tugged and pulled on the handle of the top drawer of the bureau with a newly found strength born of desperation. The wheeled bureau fell toward Samuels, then keeled over and crashed to the floor. Drawers flew open and medical supplies popped out. Twisting and turning, Samuels forced his wheelchair to tip over before Bruno could stop him. On the floor, with one wheelchair wheel spinning like mad, Samuels reached out with one hand blindly searching for anything, which might help him. It was only a moment before an enraged Bruno righted the wheelchair and gave Samuels a vicious slap across the face. Spitting out the words, he said, "We go to the roof now, Herr Samuels."

He didn't notice the small surgical knife Samuels had palmed.

Amazingly, Bruno more carried Samuels than wheeled him to the elevator, which took all of them to the roof. As they did, Samuels found the past again invading the present. Once more he was on the bridge of the *Aaron Ward* off Okinawa with a Jap kamikaze bearing down on the ship. And again, he was in Mountain Lake Park with two men choking the life out of him. Two events, each separated by many years, both causing him to relive desperate, two life-threatening moments in his life. But there was something more, a poorly disguised message to his brain, "Samuels survive."

They reached the roof an existed the elevator. Once there, Dr. Hoffman, who was still rubbing his sore shins, barked out a command. "Bruno, roll our guest to the edge. Let's see how he likes the view three stories up."

Samuels didn't like the view at all.

"For the last time," the doctor asked menacingly, where is the photo?"

Samuels considered his situation in a heartbeat. If he told his captors what they wanted to know, he would end up on the concrete below, a dead patient who had a terrible accident. On the other hand, if he remained mum, the pavement still awaited him. Death, it seemed, was the new constant in his life.

"Herr Samuels...?"

Robert Samuels decided to tell the truth.

"I mailed it, both the photo and the negative. By now, they are in safely in Washington."

"You what?" a furious Bruno sputtered, saliva spitting out of his mouth. You did what?"

"Besides being big as a gorilla are you also deaf?" Samuels asked. "I knew you were dumb, but deaf and dumb, well that takes the cake," he blurted out.

Before Dr. Hoffman could stop him, Bruno took another shot at his hostage. He hit Samuels with a withering sharp slap against the face. It was exactly what Samuels wanted. Once more Sir Isaac Newton came to his rescue. Bruno's blow, combined with Samuels' efforts to shift his weight away from his tormentor, caused the wheelchair to tip over on its side. It landed next to an air conditioning unit. The now out-of-control Bruno tried to literally pick up the wheelchair and Samuels. His strength was beyond belief. Samuels felt the wheelchair lifting off the roof. In a wild attempt to stop this, he grasped a metal pipe, which fed water to the air conditioning unit. He hung on for dear life.

Bruno would have none of it. A fist, big as a bowling ball and feeling about the same, smacked into Samuels' jaw. Reflexively, Samuels let go of the pipe. Gasping in pain, Samuels slashed out instinctively with the small surgical knife, aiming only for snarling face inches away from him. He missed the devilish face. Bruno twisted and turned at the last moment to get a better grip on the wheelchair. Samuels' apparently errant thrust caught Bruno in the leg. Blood immediately spouted from a gash in the monster's leg and onto Samuels' face. The big man howled with pain, even as he attempted to snatch the implement away from Samuels' death-like grip.

That's when Bruno made his fatal mistake.

Bruno's face came again within Samuels' reach. Without thinking Samuels impaled the knife into Bruno's face, catching his left eye. Twisting the knife with all his strength, Samuels with the last of his strength carved out the eye cavity. Blood spewed out covering both men with still more of the syrupy stuff. A glistening retina fell on Samuels. Grasping at his wound, the blinded Bruno stood up, stumbled, and then careened off the roof, and, screaming all the way, before finally crashing into the concrete below with a sickening thud.

An out-of-breath Samuels, now fighting to extricate himself from the wheelchair before Dr. Hoffman turned on him, heard sirens blaring somewhere in the city. He fought unsuccessfully at the restraining belt still holding him to the wheelchair.

"It's no good, Herr Samuels. Stop struggling."

Dr. Hoffman held a wicked looking Luger. To Samuels, the barrel seemed as large as the guns of the *USS Missouri*.

"We have reached the end, Herr Samuels."

On his side and covered in blood, Samuels tried one last thing to save himself. What he was about to do, he had seen done many times on the silver screen. With all his might he threw the surgical knife at Hoffman, hoping to imbed it in the man's chest. His aim was true, but unlike a Hollywood scene where good triumphs over evil, the knife, having hit his adversary handle first, bounced off and fell harmlessly to the roof floor.

Samuels felt like crying. He didn't want to die. He wanted to be with his wife and kids again. He wanted to pursue stories for the

Chronicle. He wanted to write his book about the Four Chaplains. He wanted another chance at life. Once more he was on the *Dorchester's* deck watching the Chaplains and Big Hit hand out their life preservers to fearful soldiers, and then again he was on the bridge of the *Aaron Ward* and a Zero was diving on the ship. His thoughts screamed at him. He needed a savior. He called out to God to intervene. He was ready to deal. He was ready to believe. He cried out in lonely desperation, "God, please save me!"

He watched as Dr. Hoffman raised the Luger.

"The sirens are quite close now, Herr Samuels. The police will be here soon. Everything is over, I'm afraid. I'm too old for the comforts of a Cologne prison. No matter... Others will follow. Our destiny will be fulfilled. Herr Samuels. It's time to say goodbye."

Then, to Samuels' complete surprise, Dr. Hoffman calmly fired one bullet into his own brain and fell undisturbed into a quiet heap on the roof.

Samuels watched all this, as if in a trance, and then, as if in slow motion, released himself to the heavens and gently collapsed on the roof, the wheelchair still securely fastened to him.

Moments later, INTERPOL found him.

CHAPTER 28

A MIRACLE AT SEA

LATE DECEMBER – SAN FRANCISCO

A few months had passed since Samuels looked into the face of death and lived to tell. After telling his tale to the CIA, INTERPOL, and the FBI, Samuels returned home to a bit of a hero's welcome. Considering what he had been through, he shined to it. A little ego polishing never hurt anyone, he thought, unless your name was Dr. Hoffman.

The intervening time had worked well for him. At home, physical and mental exhaustion were replaced by a new energy to finish his stories for the *Chronicle* and to complete his book for the Kennedys. Supported by his family and friends, he threw himself into these tasks.

By December, three more articles for the newspaper were published. One dealt with the *U-223* survivors. Kurt Roser and Gerhard Buske. The second one focused on the ever-present danger of fascist fanatics, who would destroy our democratic traditions in the name of some far-fetched racial purity. The third article, more philosophical in nature, peered into the notion of good and evil, and what it meant to have the "courage of your convictions" in order to support a moral society based on mutual respect and emphatic justice.

The entire series of *Chronicle* stories and commentaries made him a favorite for another Pulitzer Prize nomination.

As to the book about the Four Chaplains, Samuels completed the first draft by December, two months before the 20th anniversary of the *Dorchester* tragedy. His publisher promised to have the book out by January 3rd, assuming there were no additional changes. After some discussion, a title had been approved, *A Miracle at Sea*. The President of the United States would receive the first copy, autographed, of course, by the author.

Prior to publication, those who saw the dedication found the book's dedication surprising:

I dedicate this book to all the young men, both German and American, who, when asked to sacrifice their days of youth in the naval struggle for control the North Atlantic, did so with uncommon valor and our undying admiration for their dedication to family and country. May their brave souls rest, by the grace of the Almighty, in eternal peace beneath the seven seas, their struggles over.

In his introduction, Samuels teased and challenged his readers with his closing words:

It was not possible to determine with absolute certainty that Big Hit, also known as Morris Jones, was the Fifth Chaplain. The grainy black and white photograph provided by two German survivors of the U–223 does not offer conclusive evidence.

Laborious analysis by naval experts suggests only one thing. Five men were clustered together a moment before the ship descended into history. Based on my research, I have concluded that Morris Jones, a Negro cook aboard the Dorchester, exhibited the temperament, conviction, and behavior of a chaplain in the ship's last moments, and deserves to be honored as an Immortal Chaplain. In the absence of final and full empirical evidence, I find myself trusting in my instincts as a reporter and researcher, and, therefore, I am willing to make this leap of faith.

He added:

I would be remiss if I didn't include testimonies provided by the survivors of the Dorchester tragedy. They help, I think, to put everything in perspective, both in the lives lost long ago, or in our lives today.

John F. Garey, Survivor

It impressed me clearly in my mind that these chaplains demonstrated unsurpassed courage and heroism when they willingly gave their life belts to four enlisted men who, because of the utter confusion and disorder brought about by the torpedoing, had become hysterical... They helped save the lives of many of the troops.

Joseph D. Haymore, Survivor

I made for the life raft to which I was assigned and.... Passed four chaplains. One of them possessed a life jacket and other three did not. As I passed I noticed the chaplain with the life jacket remove his jacket and give it to a soldier who did not have a life jacket. I overheard the soldier say, "Thank you, Chaplain."

William J. Pantall, Survivor

From my position as I clung to a lifeboat, I saw the chaplains clearly standing at the rail of the transport minus their life jackets, urging men to leave the ship with disregard to their own safety."

Anonymous

I saw this Negro helping the captain on deck. He was handing out life jackets and spare gloves. I was quite near him before I jumped overboard. I heard him singing or maybe he was praying --- "Oh, Lord, I'm a com'in ... Make way for another poor soul..."

It was expected that there would be considerable debate about Big Hit, some joyously supportive, terribly mean-spirited with ugly racial undertones. Politicians, being the survival creatures they are when confronted with a controversy, would work the debate to their own ends, and for the most part, on a civil basis. In general, though, it was hoped most people would be fair-minded and applaud the actions of Morris Jones. And lastly, it was hoped few eyes blink when the White House recommended a new Immortal Chaplains stamp with five figures on it.

Now with Christmas just a few days away, Samuels was in his own living room with family and friends, reviewing with them a final reckoning for the very dramatic year. A newly cut Christmas tree, ringed with tinfoil and draped with an assortment of bulbs, dazzled with blinking lights. Around the tree on a white cotton blanket were many presents wrapped tightly in Christmas paper and ribbon, and, of course, taped to each present were bows of every color. It was a complete Norman Rockwell setting.

On the living room wall near the tree was a long banner with shimmering blue and white letters, which spelled out the word Hanukkah, the Jewish holiday celebrating the Maccabee's rededication of the great temple in Jerusalem. By enjoying the two festivals, those gathered together in Samuels' home were rejoicing in the spirit of brotherhood and friendship, transcending, as did the Chaplains, the secularism of any one religion. In doing so they were recognizing the lasting hope of these men --- "Interfaith in Action."

Seated in the living room were friends and family engaged in generous talk spirited along by eggnog, excellent California wine, and harder stuff for those who wished to indulge. Samuels joined them.

"Let's see if I've got this right," Samuels said, "you two resigned from the FBI?"

"Early retirement was the Director's recommendation," Brady said, almost unable to hold back a hoot.

"With a big bonus and full medical coverage," Hill added.

"What are you going to do?" Lynn asked.

"Retirement isn't for us," Hill said flatly. "We going into business for ourselves with Harry."

"Private security stuff," Harry said with a knowing smile. "Covert operations are always in vogue."

"That's great," said Rachel. "When I get out of college, maybe I can work for you guys, my three new uncles?"

"Forward your resume, young lady, when you're ready," Brady said with relish.

"How about me?" Matt asked. "I'm into being a super spy."

"You will receive every consideration," Harry responded. Now what about you, Kieran? You going to be a detective, too?"

"Thinking about being a reporter."

"Besides making a model of the *Dorchester*?"

"Yes."

"Speaking of super spies, Harry, what's the latest on our friends?" Samuels asked with a chuckle in his voice.

"Slam dunk," Harry said. "Baldy, Stretch, and Nails have all been indicted and await trial, which should be in February. As to Mr. Fairfield, the 'Source,' the same fate awaits him. Of course, he no longer works for the government."

"What about Doctor Hoffman? Matt asked. Why did he kill himself?"

"We may never know," replied Brady. "Perhaps the thought of jail time was simply too much for him."

"Maybe he just wanted to die like his hero, Hitler," Rachel said. "You know, glorious suicide to avoid being captured by his enemies."

"Very possible," Hill added."

"If he was seeking martyrdom, good riddance to him," Harry said caustically. The German police are burying his last act deeper than his body."

"Well, that seems to wrap things up as far as I can tell," Lynn said. "Isn't that so, Mr. Kurtz?"

As always, the elderly representative of the White House picked his words carefully before speaking.

"To a degree… Hoover had no choice but to put pressure on the KKK and, I must admit, he's doing a fair job. The Attorney-General is sending US Marshalls into the South to enforce integration rulings by the courts. That will not be an easy job or necessarily a peaceful one. But the Justice Department is committed. And one other thing, Mr. Samuels… The President, you should know, was delighted with your work. He's even spoken to me about a place for you in his administration, a kind of in-house historian to chronicle his life and times in the White House."

"Wow, dad, that's fantastic," Rachel said with obvious happiness.

"Before we get too far ahead of ourselves," Kurtz said in a sage voice dripping with wisdom, "I have one question."

"And that is?" Lynn asked.

"Well, if these three sleuths," he said, pointing at Hill, Brady, and Harry, are uncles, "does that at least make me a grandfather?"

"A really cool grandfather," Matt said with glee.

"My sentiments, too," Rachel piped in with equal joy.

"Me, too," Kieran added. "I've gained uncles, an aunt, and now a grandfather. That's fantastic."

"A grandfather by consensus, it would seem," Lynn said.

Robert Samuels found himself avoiding the conversation. His mind was wandering. He couldn't keep his eyes off the blinking Christmas lights on the beautiful tree. He was thinking of other blinking lights adrift in the unforgiving waters of the North Atlantic, and to men of faith, who transcended the tragedy of the *Dorchester* in the name of a glorious, living God of love.

Robert Samuels went to sleep late that night content he had fulfilled journalistic duties, as well as those of the heart. And then the phone rang just before sunrise.

CHAPTER 29

THE FORGOTTEN SAILOR

A MOMENT LATER

"Repeat that again, Kurtz."

"The report was waiting for me when I got to my motel."

"And it's been checked out?"

"The Justice Department spent three days. It's clean."

"How could we miss this?"

"Let me read the accompanying letter. It explains all."

Mr. Kurtz,

My name is Robert Anderson. I was the EX aboard the USS Comanche on February 3, 1943 when the USTS Dorchester was sunk by the U-224. With other members of our crew, I participated in rescuing as many survivors as possible. As you know, it was difficult and dangerous work, and rewarding in that we saved close to 100 men.

Recently I read Mr. Robert Samuels' series on the "Fifth Chaplain." For the first time I more fully understand what happened that night through his research. With that in mind, I would like to bring certain additional information to then White House, which I believe should be included in Samuels' reporting. Please note that I have not shared most of this information with anyone else.

My sworn statement concerning the actions of Charles W. David, a black cook aboard the USS Comanche during the rescue operation is enclosed.

"You've read the statement, Kurtz?"

"Yes."

"How does it strike you?"

"Credible in every aspect, Samuels."

"I'll be able to review it?"

"A currier will bring a copy to you today."

"Any recommendations?"

"Two. First, pause the publication of your book. Next, consider whether or not to include this material in it, as well as a story in the *Chronicle*."

"These options are okay with the White House?"

"Subject to a review of any written statement, or chapter inclusion in the book, yes."

"And you, what are your feelings?"

"Tell this guy's story."

As promised, a currier arrived at Samuels' home in the early afternoon. A thick package was exchanged for a signature. Samuels immediately went into the kitchen where Lynn and the kids waited for him. Believing that they should know about this information, he had confided in them earlier.

"That's the package," Rachel asked.

"Appears so."

"That could change the 'Fifth Chaplain' story?" Matt inquired.

"Quite possibly."

"And we get to decide?" Kieran remarked.

"Your input is needed, yes."

"Then we should get at it, Robert, don't you think so?"

"I do, Lynn."

Charles W. David

As the EX on the *Comanche*, I knew this man as well as anyone on the ship. David was a tall man, standing over six feet in height and weighing more than 200 pounds. He was very muscular, so very strong. Those robust qualities would acquit him well the night of the torpedo attack. His size could put people off. Until they got to know him, most of his shipmates were intimidated by his physical presence. In time, however, they found him to be exceptionally friendly and helpful, a guy you could count on when things got tough.

"What's an EX, Uncle Bob?"

"He's the Executive Officer on the ship, second only to the Captain, Kieran."

"How did David get into the Navy?"

"The next part of the story, Matt."

Anderson's Statement -Racism in the Navy

David enlisted in the Coast Guard prior to Pearl Harbor and was eventually placed on a Cutter, the *USS Comanche*. The Navy at that time had certain hard and fast policies concerning black sailors. Negroes were forced to take a menial position aboard a ship. In David's case that meant working in the kitchen. In additional to his other jobs, his chief responsibility was to keep the coffee hot and everyone's cup full, especially the officers. He did this job and related kitchen work with dispatch and without a complaint. This, I should add, was the Navy's hard and fast custom with black sailors board a mainly white ship with many of the crews from the South. By our standards today, this custom was discriminatory and prejudicial on the basis of race.

Whatever his personal thoughts about this situation, David kept them to himself. Certainly, as later events showed, he was a quick-thinking man of innate intelligence who acted with great courage in the best traditions of the Navy when he was required to do so. At the time, and perhaps even to this day, full integration and equal opportunities in the Navy were years in the future. In the meantime, David made so, a dignified sailor who did his job without fanfare.

As to his personal life... He was born on June 20, 1917 and was raised in New York City. After graduating from high school, he worked at numerous jobs in depression-era America before marrying his love, Kathleen, and starting a family with the son, Neil. Joining the Coast Guard promised a steady income, which was so important wen millions were still unemployed and where racism in the workplace existed. For David the Coast Guard job would be his best and last job.

Anderson's Statement - The USS Comanche's Experiment

Prior to the war, the ship was used by the Coast Guard to work the Great Lakes. It patrolled Lake Superior in particular. Because America was sort on destroyers when the war broke out, the ship was transferred to the Atlantic, where it escorted troopships to England and North Africa. Of course, blue water duty was different than the Great Lakes. No submarines lurked in the fresh water ponds.

While patrolling Lake Superior, the Coast Guard experimented with different ways to retrieve half-frozen men from icy waters, when they were unable to climb onto a life raft or pull themselves up a cargo net attached to the side of the ship. What emerged through trial and error was an old option brought up to date. A sailor dressed in a rubber suit to ward off the cold would enter the water to assist men near death. A rope would be attached to the sailor to keep him from being washed away. Though practices were held, no one ever anticipated or was prepared for hundreds of men in need, particularly at night and in a war zone.

"I wonder if the cook was trained to do this?" Matt asked.

"Anderson is mute on this question."

"If others were trained, he must have observed the practice, don't you think so?"

"A reasonable conclusion, Rachel."

"But he did go into the water after the *Dorchester* was torpedoed?"

"It's a matter of record, Lynn."

Anderson's Statement - The Record

The official record indicates that David volunteered to go into the water numerous times and contributed to saving close to a hundred men from the *Dorchester*. I can bear witness to this. He did so with only a rope tied around his body and clad only in his regular, un-insulated clothes. David and others found themselves in a race against time because of the freezing water and the eight to ten-foot high waves.

David and others had to climb down a forty-foot cargo net and then swim to the lifeboat drifting nearby, where they then assisted nearly dead men to the cutter. It was exhausting work. They had to tie ropes around the waists of men in the water because most were suffering from hypothermia and could not grab a rescue line. The record states, and I again attest to its truthfulness, that David in particular showed great physical strength, highly competent thinking, and bravery above and beyond the call of duty. All this was pointed out in my later testimony before the Navy Board of Inquiry.

David saved many men that night. He was a tower of strength. He just kept going after survivors. He was relentless. I don't know how he did it, saving so many. I was one of them. Let me make that abundantly clear. I was trying to save a drowning soldier. He was out of his mind with fear. He had a near death grip on me as he locked his arms around my neck and was threatening to drown both of us.

David was able to pull me loose from the soldier. If he hadn't, I would have died. Sadly, we could not save the soldier.

"That's some story, Uncle Bob. He saved so many people."

"He did, Kieran, but at a terrible price."

"What are you getting at, Robert?" Lynn asked, already fearful of what the answer might be.

Anderson's Statement - Greenland

When the *Comanche* arrived in Greenland and delivered the survivors to the base hospital, David was included. Days before the rescue operation, he had a raspy cough, and due to his exposure in the frigid water and subfreezing temperatures, he contracted hypothermia. He was bedridden with pneumonia and within a few weeks this powerful man succumbed to the illness. He died exactly fifty-four days after the *Dorchester* ordeal on March 29, 1943. He was twenty-six years old. It was weeks later before the crew of the *Comanche* found out about his death. There is a final ironic postscript to this story. For many years his family thought David had been buried at sea. Actually, he had been buried in Greenland. After the war, however, his remains were reinterred in the Long Island National Cemetery at Farmdale, Long Island. Apparently, his family was never told. For decades the family lived in New York City, within a few miles of Charles W. David's final resting place. Almost sixty years later, the Navy undertook a systematic search for his immediate family, and for other seamen and their families. Once notified, David's family finally knew where he was buried with honors.

"Dad, that all seems so unfair."

"Fairness is always illusive when the world is at war."

"Was his heroics at least played up in the newspapers?"

"In the Negro Press, yes, Lynn. Beyond that, not much was said. It wasn't that he was written out of history. More that he sort of disappeared into it waiting for a day when he might be rediscovered."

"Is that day now?" Matt asked.

"Meaning?"

"Are you going to include David in the *Chronicle* series about the *Dorchester*?"

"I think you should," Kieran stated directly. "He earned a place."

"Talk about a "Sixth Chaplain?"

"Or maybe equal reflections of the "Fifth Chaplain," Lynn said. "That's possible, isn't it?"

"Let me tell you too more things, Anderson included in his statement. Then we'll decide as a family. Okay?"

Anderson's Statement –Merit and Honors

I'll never forget the night the *Dorchester* was sunk. However, another date also comes to mind. It was June 21, 1944. A simple ceremony was held at the Coast Guard Headquarters. Rear Admiral Thomas Parker presented David's wife and three-year old son with the Navy and Marine Corp medal for his bravery. I was honored to be present. The ceremony described David as a man who saved others with his sheer, raw courage and his great strength. Admiral Parker read the official citation, which in part noted that David's "great courage and unselfish perseverance contributed to the saving of many lives and were in keeping with the highest traditions of the United States Naval Service." I added a few words: "David's bravery was an inspiration to every officer and man on the cuter."

I later learned that the Immortal Chaplains Foundation established years later awarded David its first "Prize for Humanity," which honors those who risk their lives for a person ;of another faith or race. David, I might add, shared the "Prize" with Desmond Tutu of South Africa who was honored for his opposition to apartheid.

Personal Statement

What follows is my personal statement and does not necessarily represent the official U.S. Navy position.

The present USPO postal stamp commemorating the "Four Immortal Chaplains" is special for all the obvious reasons. The White House's effort to locate a possible "Fifth Chaplain" is worthy, political interests notwithstanding. If Big Hit is the missing chaplain, so be it, and a new stamp should be printed. But let us also consider the case of Charles W. David for that honor.

The "Immortal Chaplains" were men of faith. They had taken vows. In many ways they were children of the *Holy Bible*. They were motivated by a belief in a loving, just God, but what about Big Hit and David? They had taken no religious vows. Whatever their religious beliefs, they were personal. Whatever motivated them to save others had little to, I believe, with formal religious training, or their conception of a deity. To degree, the Four Immortal Chaplains were expected to act as they did on the *Dorchester*, but not necessarily Big Hit. The same was true for David on the *USS Comanche*. David could, if he so decided, leap into the cruel sea again and again, but he was not required by Naval custom or a "higher institutional morality." So why did the two Negro cooks act as they did?

I believe this to be the case. They weren't motivated by what others thought or expected. Rather, it was what they expected of themselves that counted. I believe they acted as they did to prove to others that they were men deserving to be treated fairly in the Navy. They were more than cooks and wanted others to understand this. They, I believe felt they should not be relegated to kitchen service simply on the basis of color. They were proud men and competent sailors in the Coast Guard. They were as good as any other man. They wanted to be treated as an equal with respect due all sailors. The *Dorchester* disaster provided them with an opportunity to show their grit and merit.

I believe there was still more involved. By their actions, Big Hit and David were challenging the racist attitudes and discriminatory practices of their day. They were proving, I think, the bigots wrong as they pushed against the wrongs done to Negroes. But they were also acknowledging their faith in America that segregation could be overcome. In some ways, they were repudiating the so-called Draftee's Prayer, which appeared in the Negro press in January 1943:

> Dear Lord, today
> I go to war;
> To fight, to die,
> Tell me what for?
> Dear Lord, I'll fight,
>
> I do not fear
> Germans and Japs;
> My fears are here,
> America!

I conclude with this. It's been said that facts are stubborn things. They are what they are. I believe that. In the case of the Immortal Chaplains and Big Hit, they handed out their lifejackets to five men, and possibly saved their lives, five lives. David repeatedly went into the North Atlantic to rescue one man after another, possibly saving over 90 with help of ship's crew. All this has been attested to in documents I've included. If for no other reason in the terrible arithmetic of life and death, David should be honored. Numbers do count, reflecting as they do, lives saved. Therefore, I recommend that David's name should be included with the others, all chaplains in their own right.

Robert W. Anderson

"Dad, what are you going to do?"

"Before I answer that question, I want to share a quote I came across recently. It bears upon my decision. Okay?"

Before the opposition, assuming it existed, could organize, Samuels said. Adam Antigire is the grandson of Anderson. He described David's actions and sacrifice:

If I were not for Charles David my grandfather would have been left by the Comanche in the confusion and would have surely died. My understanding is that there were only a few volunteers to go into the water to attempt to save the soldiers from the Dorchester. For someone in Mr. David's position to step up and volunteer to go into the water to save those men clearly shows what kind of a person Charles David was. What a selfless act... My family and the families of the dozens of men Mr. David helped to save that evening are forever indebted to him.

"Rachel, your question might be better put this way. What have I already done?"

"And what was that?" Lynn asked, a shy smile on her face.

"A new chapter will be added to the book. David will stand tall with the others, and the *Chronicle* will carry a two-part story about Charles W. David."

CHAPTER 30

REDEMPTION

FEBRUARY 3, 1963 – KIEL, GERMANY

The two men moved slowly down the jetty toward the waters of the stormy Baltic Sea. The night air was cold, almost freezing. Because of this, they wore heavy dark blue coats, a throwback to their youthful naval days. Their coat collars were turned up to ward off the cold. Their heavy woolen caps fought the sharp winds pouring off the Baltic, as did their thick gloves.

Each carried a large wreath made up of pine bows freshly cut for them.

At the end of the jetty, they stopped.

"We're here, Kurt."

"Yes, Gerhard."

The two men gazed out at the Baltic. A sense of sadness and remorse clung to them.

"Herr Samuels wrote a good book, Gerhard."

"He did. He's a good reporter and decent man."

"He did well by the *U – 223*," Kurt said.

"And by the *Dorchester*."

"It's time, Kurt?"

"Yes."

The man called Kurt looked out over the jetty and gently tossed his wreath into the water below. As he did, he said, "May a just God have mercy on their souls, our shipmates of the *U – 223*."

The second man, Gerhard, then dropped his wreath into the water, saying, "May the light of the Almighty shine upon the *Dorchester's* souls."

Having completed their task, the two men watched the wreaths floating in the water aware of another dark night. They remained silent knowing that words were beyond what they felt.

At last the two men turned and retraced their steps back across the jetty. As they did, Kurt asked his companion, "Gerhard, do you think Herr Samuels ever realized what we did?"

"No. The photo I gave him was of another ship, but he could not know that."

"He so needed to believe in a Fifth Chaplain."

"As do we, Kurt."

CHAPTER 31

EPILOGUE

The tragedy of the USAT Dorchester and the sacrifice of the Four Chaplains has been acknowledged and remembered in any number of ways by Americans, who honor bravery and courage, when extraordinary men make the ultimate sacrifice to protect others. All of us shine in their light.

In 1948, the Four Chaplains were awarded Purple Hearts and the Distinguish Service Cross. The award was made posthumously to the families of the chaplains.

In the same year, the United States Post Office, throwing tradition to the wind, printed the famous Four Immortal Chaplains stamp only five years after their deaths.

In 1951, the Chapel of the Four Chaplains was established in Philadelphia on what is now the campus of Temple University. The funding came from Clark Poling's father, Daniel Poling. President Harry S. Truman spoke at the dedication. He emphasized the "unity of our country" as a larger "unity under God."

In 1961, a special medal was authorized by the Congress to honor the Four Chaplains, the Congressional Medal of Valor. It was by design the equivalent of the Congressional Medal of Honor and cannot be awarded again.

In the 1960's, the town of Dorchester in Clark County, Wisconsin, erected a simple monument to the Four Chaplains. In a park stones were placed in a small pile with a portion of a black anchor. Placed in the stone pile was a plaque to remember the *USAT Dorchester*.

In York, Pennsylvania, the Alexander Goode Elementary School was established in the 1970's. In the school's lobby there is a ceramic likeness of the chaplains. Identical inscriptions from Malachi 2:10 (Old Testament) are found in the memorial in three languages, Hebrew (Rabbi Goode), Latin (Father Washington) and English (George Fox and Clark Poling). The quote reads:

> *Have we not all one Father?*
> *Hath not one God created us?*
> *Why do we deal treacherously every man against his*
> *brother,* by profaning the covenant of our fathers?

The great ship, the *Queen Mary*, sits in Long Beach, California. A sanctuary dedicated to the Four Chaplains is in this ship, which ironically, carried POW survivors to the United States from the doomed *U – 223*.

In 1997, the Immortal Four Chaplain Foundation was established on the campus of Hamlin University in St. Paul, Minnesota. Three of its founders included David Fox, nephew of Chaplain George Fox; Rosalie Goode-Fried, the daughter of Alexander Goode; and Theresa Goode, his wife.

The Foundation's mission statement is to "tell their uplifting story and the stories of people who have also risked everything to save others of another faith or ethnicity and to remind us of the capacity for compassion we all have in us." In this spirit, the Immortal Chaplains Prize for Humanity is given to a worthy person.

One of the first awards was given to Charles W. David Jr., a black mess cook on the *USCG* Cutter *Comanche*. He died from pneumonia after repeatedly saving *Dorchester* survivors from the icy water.

The Foundation's greatest achievement occurred in 2000. Alexander Goode's widow, Theresa, was convinced by her family to invite two German *U – 223* survivors to a meeting in her Chevy Chase home in Maryland to foster reconciliation between the two countries. Two survivors attended, Kurt Roser and Gerhard Buske. Also in attendance was Ben Epstein. Though difficult, the meeting engendered what Buske called "love rather than hate." In addition, Buske spoke, saying:

We the sailors of U–223 regret the deep sorrows and pains caused by the torpedo. Wives lost their husbands, parents their sons, and children waited for their fathers in vain. I once more ask forgiveness, as we had to fight for our country, as your soldiers had to do for theirs.

He closed his remarks by urging people to emulate the examples of the chaplains:

We ought to love when others hate; e ought to forgive when others are violent.

I wish that we could say the truth to correct errors; we can bring faith where doubt threatens; we can awaken hope where despair exists; we can light up light where darkness reigns; that we can bring joy where sorrows dominate.

That is what we should do in this time of human conflict, where hate and revenge will never create peace.

Also speaking at the ceremony was Ben Epstein, who at first was very reluctant to meet with the Germans. However, he did meet. explaining:

You have got to talk and figure out what it was the caused all of these problems.

A civil rights bill was never passed during the Kennedy Administration. A single assassin's bullet ended that dream.

In 1965 the United States Congress passed the Civil Rights Act. It was done at the urging of the new president, Lyndon B. Johnson.

In retrospect, perhaps David Fox summed up the sacrifice of the Four Chaplains by reminding all of us of the Foundation's motto: "If we can die together, can't we live together?"

The question is still ours to answer.

Printed in the United States
By Bookmasters